TWELFTH GRADE HOPES AND FEARS

BRUCE INGRAM

SECANT PUBLISHING

For information about this title, contact the publisher:
Secant Publishing, LLC
615 North Pinehurst Avenue
Salisbury, MD 21801
www.secantpublishing.com

978-1-944962-65-4 (paperback)
978-1-944962-73-9 (e-book)

Library of Congress Control Number: 2020905922

This book is a work of fiction. Names, characters, businesses, places, events, and incidents are products of the author's imagination or are used in a fictitious manner. Any resemblance to actual persons, living or dead, or to actual events is purely coincidental.

Printed in the United States of America

❀ Created with Vellum

CONTENTS

A MONTH LATER

ACKNOWLEDGMENTS

The following teachers and staff for Botetourt County Schools and Lord Botetourt High School assisted with this book.

Carrie Baldacci
Rob Campbell
Jessie Curulla
Jamie Duncan
Heather Garnett
Doak Harbison
Selena Harvey
Ashley Hatcher
Kevin Hix
Whitney Hughes
Mary Lewis
Kendel Lively
Michael Martin
Christen Myers

The following students in the author's Creative Writing classes also assisted with this book.

Madelyn Badgley
Briana Barnett
Allison Coombe
Julia Garber
Kaylee Golder
Madison Gunter
McKayla Hoke
Taylor Jones
Trystan Layman
Faith Overbay
Sidney Saunders
Angel Swain
Garrett Wade

BACK TO SCHOOL

1

LUKE

I'M WILLING TO BET THAT NONE OF MY TEACHERS, WELL MAYBE Ms. Hawk, would have thought I would ever be graduating from high school when they met me as a ninth-grader. Heck, my original plans were for me to drop out as soon as I reached the legal age to quit. And here I am, not only going to graduate, but I'm going to college. I don't know where yet, but somewhere for sure.

Yeah, I hated school back then. It's still not the greatest place to be, especially any kind of math class, the cafeteria, the bathrooms, just about any science class, the bullying, Spanish class when we have to read out loud. Getting tutored in math for the state tests...well, that was pretty bad...plus all those *Fs* and *Ds* in Algebra and Geometry. No more state tests for me now because I'm a senior. It's weird. Senior year is the year when the state should have the most interest in what we know before we "go off into the world." Instead, the state is obsessed that some ninth-grader somewhere might not know what a metaphor is, or who is buried in Grant's Tomb, or when the War of 1812 took place. I'm still waiting for the day when I use my newfound "geometry skills" from tenth grade.

But I survived all that, and I survived Mom dying from

cancer and later Dad getting killed in a car wreck when he was drunk driving. I survived Mia having to break up with me when we were sophomores because her dad told her to, and I survived all the ups and downs of dating all these other girls and relationships that never went anywhere. I don't have a girlfriend now, and I'm not looking to do much dating if any this year. The only girl besides Mia I was ever really interested in was Elly, and she turned me down the two times I asked her out last year. I'm not going to find true love in high school, that's for sure. Who really does, anyway?

I've been living with Granddaddy since partway through my sophomore year when I ran away from home because Dad was drinking so hard and was so abusive after Mom's death. But now one of my biggest fears is that Granddaddy will have to go to a nursing home, or worse. He must have dementia or Alzheimer's or something. He can't remember anything anymore. Granddaddy hasn't driven since last year sometime. I hide the keys to our pickup so he can't. He keeps asking me when I will be 18, and I keep saying December 10, and he keeps forgetting. Sometimes I fear that the only thing that is keeping him alive is me saying that I'm not 18 yet. That somehow he thinks I'll be put in foster care if he dies.

I was really worried about that, too, so when I went to get my schedule, I finally broke down and told Mrs. Whitney, my guidance counselor, about Granddaddy's condition and asked if I would have to go to a foster home if he died.

"Luke, why didn't you come to me about this before? I would've been glad to have helped you," she said. "No, Social Services is not going to put you in foster care because you're so close to being 18. But because you're so close to being an adult, they're not going to do anything to help you out, either. I'm not being harsh; that's just the reality of it."

Then Mrs. Whitney said she could help me by contacting Social Services, and she did. Right there in her office, she arranged for somebody to come by our house and make an assessment about Granddaddy. This woman came by, and it didn't take her long to realize that I needed help taking care of him. I've been having to put those adult diapers on him every morning because sometimes he forgets to go to the bathroom, especially at night or when I'm at school. Next week when school starts, Granddaddy will be spending part of every day at an adult day care center. Social Services is even arranging for a van to pick him up and bring him home. That's a load off me. It's been tough taking care of him by myself, plus doing all the grocery shopping, bill paying, and house stuff. I'm not much of a cook. I mean I can heat water and dump stuff in it, but not much more than that.

I had to look through Granddaddy's stuff to find out what bills to pay, and I found out that he did a wonderful thing for me. He bought that 30 acres of land out in the country that we looked at a couple years ago. I don't know when he did that. I can go build a house one day and live there. Granddaddy must have taken the inheritance money from Mom and Dad, plus what he had saved up to be able to buy the land. I know it was hard for him to have done that with the only money coming in for him being his pension and his Social Security checks.

I can use the money I've saved from working and hoarding every last penny for college. It won't even be enough to pay for my freshman year of college, but it's a start. I saved all I could from my summer job as a janitor. What an awful job: cleaning toilets, coming in early to remove the grease from around the grill, washing the windows multiple times day after day, taking loads of trash to the dumpster, and picking up all this crap from the parking lot because people are too pathetic to walk two steps to a trash bin. I'm so done with that job.

I ran a lot over the summer, especially with Marcus. I'm hoping to have a great cross-country season and maybe get some sort of athletic scholarship for that. Maybe I can get some sort of financial aid because, well, because of my money situation. I also want to get my GPA up from 2.4. It's the highest it's ever been, but maybe I can raise it a little more, and some college will give me a look...hopefully the local small college. I could be a day student and save money from not living in a dorm.

Yeah, I'm going to go to college and become a teacher and make something of myself. I'm tired of feeling scared and poor. I know I've got a chip on my shoulder about this, and I want to get rid of that chip. I want to have more hope than fear in my life.

2

ELLY

I REALLY LIKED WORKING AT MY PARENTS' COUNTRY CLUB THIS summer, especially reading to little kids during story time. I feel like I did a good job, and being with those kids confirmed that I've made the right choice to be an elementary school teacher when I graduate from college. I tried to read very expressively, and the kids really responded to me with lots of giggles and questions.

I didn't do such a great job with the outdoor recreation stuff —the nature walks and creek stomps. That time Luke came over and helped me identify some plants and animals was a little helpful, but I didn't know much more than the little kids I was leading around. So many times I wanted to call Luke and ask him to give me some more advice on what to cover or come help me out or come as a guest speaker. But I never could call him, no matter how much I wanted to.

I should have gone out with him when he asked me those two times last year. He would have been so good and right for me instead of Caleb and all those other guys I've gone out with during my high school years. The physical and emotional abuse I put up with from Caleb...why did I stay with him for so long when he was so cruel to me about my not being thin enough or

—pretty enough—not being good enough for him. Forcing myself to throw up so that I could look the way he wanted me to. Was I one of those girls who was too stupid, too desperate to be with a certain type of guy... the popular, sexy, drop-dead gorgeous guy... that I couldn't think straight? I'm afraid I know the answer to that question.

Well, if I've learned anything from dating in high school, it's that type of guy is not the type that you want to spend the rest of your life with. My parents thought Caleb was Mr. Wonderful, so did some of my friends. I should have listened to good friends like Mia, Paige, and Kylee, who warned me from the start about Caleb. They know what kind of a person he is deep down. I'm through with boys like Caleb. I'm going to follow my heart and my head from now on.

I know in my heart that I want a sweet, kind boy. I know that I want a man who will be my life partner and my equal, And I know that there's only one boy at my high school that meets those requirements...Luke. This year, I'm going to show him that I'm the right girl for him. We'll be working together on Yearbook assignments in Ms. Hawk's class, and we'll probably be at least in the same English 12 Honors and U.S. Government Honors classes, so I will have plenty of opportunities for him to see that I care about him. That I'm worth having as a girlfriend, maybe even somebody that he could love.

The thing I'm really worried about is that no matter how hard I go after him, he won't give me another chance. I worry that he'll just feel that I'm being so kind to him because we've known each other for so long. What should I do if that's the case? Should I actually ask him out? My parents, Dad especially, don't like Luke because of his background and his father's run-ins with the law. If Luke and I started dating, would we have to do it in secret? What would my Dad do if he ever found out?

I don't know what to do. I really can't ask Mia for advice because deep down I think she really wants to get back together with him because they were together for almost two years. I obviously can't go to Mom for help, either. And I can't go to

Paige or Kylee because they're such good friends with Mia. I'm all twisted up in knots about this. If I hesitate and do nothing and Luke gets back together with Mia or finds some other girl to love,...I'd never forgive myself for not trying to be with him. I've got to make a decision.

I'm almost certain I'm going to the local small college. I've got a 3.8 GPA, so my grades are plenty good enough for me to be accepted. The college is only 12 miles from our house. Mom and Dad said they'd pay for me to live on campus, even though I could easily drive there every day. They said that living in a dorm would be a good experience for me and help me learn more about myself and the viewpoints of people from around the country. They're right about all that. But my living on campus does seem to be a waste of money. They've pampered me my whole life because I'm the oldest of their three children and the only girl.

Thank goodness I've grown up enough now to handle being away at college. At least, I hope I have. The only good thing about going out with all those high school jerks is I've definitely learned how to identify a loser guy. If I hadn't, I'd probably fall into the wrong crowd the first week of being away at college. I finally know and really, really believe that I've got my head on straight now. I know who I am and what I want out of life. I'm going to have a great senior year, make the *A* honor roll, get ready for college and my life after. Maybe even go after the boy who is right for me.

3

MARCUS

WORKING AS A SCRIBE AT THE MUSEUM OVER THE SUMMER WAS a real eye-opener for me. I know now I've had it much better than most black guys my whole life. How the hard work and sacrifices that both sets of grandparents made were carried down to my parents and my older brother Joshua and me. Growing up in a mostly upper-class neighborhood was something I always took for granted. I won't anymore. No wonder my parents were always on my case, especially when I was a freshman and had a sucky attitude.

The thing that really made all that clear to me was reading those letters from World War I and II black soldiers during the summer. The museum had asked me to read and type up the letters that local servicemen had sent home. Mrs. Jennings, the curator, is going to put those letters into a coffee-table-type book with pictures of these local men and women in uniform back in the day.

I was really angry about what those black soldiers went through. In World War I, they mostly weren't allowed to serve in combat because they were considered to be too stupid and cowardly to possibly perform well in battle. So they did a lot of slave-style manual labor. They were also racially segregated from the other troops, and their clothes, training, and everything else was substandard. Reading those letters that those guys sent home was just awful—the pain they felt. One soldier wrote about one of his best friends being lynched when they were in training—the guy had done something really bad—walking at night while black.

I read letters from World War II soldiers where it was obvious that the soldiers were still being treated like dirt. I had already known that the troops were still segregated then, but I didn't realize how bad it was even in the 1940s. The American military even tried to enforce Jim Crow laws when the men were overseas in Europe. With all that was going on and trying to defeat the Nazis and Japanese, what sense did it make to waste time and money on Jim Crow? I already had learned in Mr. Martin's history class that Hitler had looked upon America's Jim Crow system as "ideal." But I had no idea it was that bad until I read those letters.

I told Mrs. Jennings everything I was finding out, and she suggested that I read a book on the subject, *Taps for a Jim Crow Army: Letters from Black Soldiers in World War II*. Man, it was something—what those soldiers went through, fighting the enemy for the sake of "freedom" and not being treated like human beings when they weren't on the battlefield.

I also e-mailed Mr. Martin over the summer to see if I should load up on history classes for this year. I'm having him for U.S. Government Honors and Mr. Wayne for American Conflicts. They're two of my favorite teachers, and I know they'll get me ready for college history classes. Mr. Martin also told me to change my schedule so that I could take World Religions. He sent this detailed e-mail on why I should.

"Marcus, we have an expanding global world, but at the same time, it's shrinking. I know that sounds like a paradox, and it is. The larger the world population grows, the smaller the world becomes in terms of our communications digitally and through social media with each other. To be an educated person today, you have to know about the cultures and religions of other people around the globe. That's why I think you should take World Religions, because so much of how many countries react to certain issues today is tied to their religious beliefs. For example, most Americans don't know why Sunni and Shia Muslims hate each other, but they should, to understand the Middle East."

I spent a lot of time running with Luke, many mornings when it was still dark. I'm glad he brought up about my running cross-country. I'm never going to get back all my old speed and explosiveness because of my ACL injury. But I'm going to try to get as much of it back as possible so I'll be ready for basketball season. I get to be a walk-on for the state university my freshman year there with the promise of a scholarship if I perform well. My leg hardly ever hurts from the surgery anymore. I just have to be real careful and slow about warming up.

It was weird not going to summer football practice for the first time since like forever. I didn't know when it happened, but the concussion and leg injury I had as a sophomore were the end of my being a good football player. I'm not going to replay in my head anymore what went wrong when I was injured. It's time for me to move on and leave football behind.

I didn't have a lot of time to spend with my girlfriend Camila over the summer, but we made what time we did have count. We went to the local state park several times and went out to dinner or a movie quite a few times. My best times with her were just driving over to my house and walking in the twilight. This relationship just might last. I really want it too. She's just what I hope to have as a wife one day—a smart, no-nonsense girl that's not going to take crap off anybody, including me. But she's also somebody that has a real tender side to her that is really good for me. I think I'm starting to get my life together now.

4

MIA

IT DIDN'T TAKE MAMA LONG TO MOVE ON FROM MY FATHER, and I'm very glad she did. At the start of the summer, she began dating Dr. Sai Kumar, who Mama met at the hospital where she's a nurse. Mama's divorce won't be final until January, but I don't see any reason why she shouldn't be dating other men. My father was so domineering and bossy to Mama and me. He was the same way to my younger sisters Isabella and Emma. On one hand, I can tell that my sisters miss him. He doesn't even bother to call my younger sisters and me more than once a month. I don't mind that at all... in a way. But I think it hurts my sisters' feelings for him to be so indifferent. I haven't missed the tension that existed between Mama and him—the stress that was in our home all the time between him and us. Besides all that, he was the one that cheated on Mama and broke their marriage vows, not the other way around.

Sai, he wants us to call him by his first name; I've met him several times when he's come over to pick up Mama. He lives in the same neighborhood where Elly, Marcus, Caleb, and some of the other students at school live. Elly told me his house is like a mansion compared to even the really nice ones on her street. Sai is divorced, and he and his wife didn't have any children. If he and Mama should ever get married, I bet he's going to want children. Mama's still young enough to have more kids, but that would be weird—going to college and having a baby brother or sister around when I come home for breaks. You know that expression about "Only in America." Only in America could a poor, divorced, second-generation Mexican-American woman and her three girls go from living where we do to possibly a ritzy neighborhood with a wealthy Indian-American doctor.

I'm on track to be valedictorian of my high school class, and my class load at the local community college is going to be even more stressful than last year. For the fall semester, I have to take College Chemistry 112; ITE 115, Introduction to Computer Applications and Concepts; Philosophy 220 Ethics; and Psychology 220 – Principles. And then, complete my day with honors U.S. Government and Calculus, plus English 12 A.P. at the high school. I should be able to sleep, like, two hours a night with that load.

But I've got to work like this if I'm going to fulfill my dream of becoming a pediatrician and going back to Texas where we have family, or even moving to Mexico. I know about the poverty we came from, and I want to do something meaningful where I make the lives of people like us better. The courses will change, of course, but this type of schedule and workload will have to go on for years for me to reach that goal. I can do it. I'm not worried about that; it's just going to be exhausting and there won't be much time for a social life.

I've already got a full four-year scholarship to the state university. I guess that's one of the *perks* to likely being a valedictorian who just happens to not have any money. At least, I don't have tuition-type pressure to deal with.

Mateo and I saw each other some over the summer. He's a nice, smart guy I met at the college last year. But I don't feel anything when he kisses me, and I don't get excited when he calls or texts. Or feel down when several days go by without him contacting me. I guess we'll keep dating some this year. I admit it's nice every once in a while to do something not related to my studies—to get dressed and go out and have a guy pay for everything.

Over the summer, things were a lot less hectic, and I had a lot of time to think. I took Chemistry III like Dr. Myers, my college advisor, told me to do in order to get it out of the way, and I worked as a waitress, which was really good money with the tips and all. But outside of those things, I actually had some time to myself to read for pleasure, go walking in the evenings, and think. Every time I would go out walking, sooner or later my thoughts would turn to Luke and what might have been.

Those two years when we were together in ninth and tenth grade were probably the happiest times of my life. You could say we were just kids then, but I don't care. What we felt for each other was real and meaningful. I still miss him. I kept wanting to call him all summer and never did. When my father broke us up, all I could think of was one day getting back together with Luke.

But I have this fear that he won't want to get back together again. And I have this fear that if we did, Luke might not wait for me during all the years I had to go to college and grad school. Or want to move to Texas or Mexico with me to spend our lives. I also have this fear that I wouldn't have the strength to leave him if he refused to go.

Which member of a couple should give in if their hopes and dreams conflict? In Luke's and my case, I don't think it should be me. Why am I even thinking about all this when I haven't even called him like I promised myself a thousand times that I would before the summer even started. I'm going to call him when we get back to school and see if he wants to go have coffee or something.

BACK TO SCHOOL
CONTINUED

5

LUKE

WELL, IT WAS BACK TO THE OLD GRIND THIS WEEK. I HAVE Ms. Roche again, this time for first period English 12 A.P. We started right in with Shakespeare and *Macbeth*. She did the neatest thing before we started reading the play. She divided us into four-person groups and gave us a list of Shakespearean insults, curse words, common phrases, and vocabulary from that play and others. We had to write a play using those words and act it out in front of the class. In my other English classes, I had read *Romeo and Juliet* in ninth grade and *Hamlet* in tenth grade, so I had some familiarity with the language. But the creative way Ms. Roche introduced *Macbeth* gave us a head start on knowing words and phrases before we came across them in the actual reading.

When I become a teacher, I want to be creative like that and get the students excited. It's just so boring the way too many teachers teach. Lecture, give notes, lecture, give notes, sit up straight, stop falling asleep, put your phone away, lecture, give notes, test tomorrow. "You're going to fail the test if you don't start paying better attention!"

I mean, like, divide us into groups and let us create something on our own, have us explore some concept, and do a presentation for the class. Create a game where we have to compete against each other for extra credit. Have multiple activities every day in class; have us get up and move around and do something. Compete against another class in some activity. Bring in some guest speakers that are passionate about something we're studying. Is that too much to ask? It sure seems so.

Second period, I wasn't happy about having to pass another math class in order to graduate. Before school started on the first day, I went to Mrs. Whitney and complained about having to take Statistics. But she told me straight up that it was either that or Calculus. "And I have a feeling," she said, "after the first day of school you would be coming to me, begging to get switched to Statistics. You know, of course, that for some people Calculus is even harder than Geometry."

She's right, I would have come to complain. And she didn't have to add that I would have been one of those *some people* that find Calculus harder than Geometry. Geometry was absolutely the worse class that I've ever taken, and I want to have nothing to do with classes that are harder than that crap.

Actually, the first assignment in Statistics wasn't too bad. It absolutely floored me. My *old friend* and state test remedial tutor Mrs. Roberts is the teacher, and she said the first thing we were going to study was the laws of probability.—that we were going to have to design a long-term project where we had to determine what were the statistical chances of something happening.

At first, I was in a panic to come up with an idea for something to do. But then it hit me. I would create the statistical probability of me being successful as a deer hunter based on temperature, wind direction, food availability, stage of the deer rut and breeding cycle, and many other factors. I would keep records of all my hunts this fall and then compile the data on how many deer I saw per trip and whether I killed one or not.

Mrs. Roberts is pretty hardnose about a lot of things, and I didn't expect her to go along with my idea. But she said it was a great plan and for me to run the project during bow season and give her weekly updates on how it was going. My weekly updates could count as daily grades. I was just stunned that she went along. I mean everybody in that class is in the same boat as me—too stupid to take advanced math classes but desperate to get one last math credit to graduate. Mrs. Roberts was probably glad that I had any kind of idea at all for a project. You know, I might be able to get as high as a *D+* for this class. I've never attained such *lofty* heights as that before. Senior sarcasm, it's a thing, you know? I think it's a requirement to graduate.

Third period in U.S. Government, Mr. Martin gave us a list of topics to research as two-person teams, and Marcus and I paired up like last year and picked the "Founding Fathers' Feelings on Slavery." Next, it was time for lunch, which I skipped and headed for the library to read. I ate my usual Clif Bar without having the librarian, Mrs. Kendel, spotting me for breaking her no eating in the library rule.

Spanish droned on like usual, and the highpoint was me not having to read out loud, followed by Advanced Phys Ed (otherwise known as pickup basketball most days), Biology A.P. (it was a no brainer to choose that over Physics A.P. and all that math that goes along with it), and Yearbook. As seniors, Elly and I are co-editors. We've worked with Ms. Hawk for three years on the staff,. So Elly and I had to sit down with Ms. Hawk and work out plans for what we have to cover for the year and the schedule of when spreads should be turned in and which students should do which spreads.

Elly seemed a little strange in the way she acted toward me, both in Yearbook and earlier in English. It was like she was trying to joke around with me and tease me but couldn't quite do it. Maybe she's worried that I'm angry at her for turning me down twice for dates last year. I'm still disappointed at that, sure, but I could never be angry at her. At the end of Yearbook class, the most unexpected thing happened. Kylee came up to me and said, "Got a second?" I said yep and then she said, "I've never asked a boy out before, but I thought a lot about doing this over the summer. Would you like to come over to my house for me to cook dinner for you Friday night?"

I said yeah...not bad for a guy who wasn't planning to do much, if any, dating this year.

6

ELLY

In the past, before the first day of school, I would have spent hours agonizing and texting friends over what should I wear. After that was settled, I would go through more misery and more texts about how I should wear my hair, getting up hours earlier than I needed to, and worrying and fretting with my clothes, hair, and makeup. The goal? To get guys to notice me. How could I have been so stupid and shallow? After all, we're talking about high school boys here, not exactly the princes of the universe.

The strange thing is, I've finally realized that I do look okay... well, actually, better than just okay. I'm no longer overweight like I was as a freshman and most of my sophomore year and no longer painfully underweight from all my excessive dieting and throwing up as a junior. I've finally realized that my naturally curly brown hair, which I've let grow to being halfway down my back, suits me just fine. Mom actually had to wake me up, I was sleeping so soundly. I ate a nice healthy breakfast of orange juice and oatmeal with two bananas; put on a pair of jeans, blouse, and sweater, didn't bother with any makeup; and was ready for the day.

When I got to Ms. Roche's first period English 12 A.P. class, I saw that the seat next to Luke was vacant and sat down there. And that's when all the old doubts about myself started to resur-face. I actually stuttered when I asked him how his summer job had been and immediately realized that I had asked the wrong thing when he mumbled "cleaning toilets and filling dumpsters mixed in with picking up trash. Want to know more details?" What I should have asked is something like, "What books did you read over the summer? Did you get to go fishing much?" Then just said, matter of fact-like, "Do you want to go have coffee with me after school to talk about Yearbook and other stuff?" But I didn't, and while I was thinking about what I should say next, Ms. Roche said it was time to start.

We're beginning the year with reading *Macbeth*, and although Ms. Roche said we wouldn't be actually starting on the play until later in the week, she was going to assign parts now. She asked if anybody wanted to be Macbeth, and Luke volunteered. Then Ms. Roche said who wanted to be his wife, Lady Macbeth. I thought about volunteering for that character, but then I hesi-tated because I know this play is a Shakespearean tragedy, which means that most of the main characters die or kill each other. While I was hesitating, Kylee said she would take the role, which turned out to be just the first time that day she beat me out for something involving Luke.

Second period, I have Trigonometry so I knew Luke wouldn't be in there. Math is okay, I always get an *A* in whatever type of math I take, but I don't enjoy taking any math class. I know this is a stereotype, but I think most girls like English better than most guys, and I think most guys like math better than most girls.

I thought about getting my schedule changed to take Statistics with Luke, but I figured Caleb was in that class, too. I heard he's dropped out of all the honors classes, probably because he's taking the easy way out his senior year. Or maybe because Caleb feels he's going to party and booze his way through senior year. I don't even want to be in the same building with him, let alone a classroom.

By third period government, I had made up my mind to sit next to Luke again and bring up the coffee thing, but when I got to the room, Luke was already sitting with Marcus and Allen and talking about sports junk. During lunch, I sat with Paige, Kylee, Hannah, and my other friends as usual. Kylee announced that she was thinking about asking Luke out for a date during Year book and would that be too forward of her? Hannah told her to "go for it," which set off another round of conversations, followed by Kylee asking me what I thought. I stammered around for a while, then gave a fake smile, and said, "Do whatever you think best."

I think she knows I have a thing for Luke, but on the other hand, maybe she doesn't. During Yearbook, Ms. Hawk, Luke, and I spent most of the period working together. Subconsciously, I know I dragged out our time together to keep Kylee from having a chance to talk to him. It felt so lame making small talk. Was that wrong of me? Maybe it was, but I don't care.

At the end of class, I saw Kylee, all dressed up in a nice miniskirt and looking perfectly put together, walk up to Luke and turn on the charm. I saw him grin and nod his head. So she did ask him out, and he did say yes.

Paige and I are partnering on a government project: "Thomas Paine's Influence on the American Revolution." So that was my pretext for calling her. After we had talked about that for all of two minutes, Paige said, "That project is not the real reason you called, is it?"

"What do you mean?" I said.

"I saw you making small talk with Luke in English. I saw your face cloud over during lunch when Kylee brought up the possibility of asking Luke out," she said. "I saw your expression in Yearbook when she did walk up to him.

"Elly, that boy has it bad for you. I can tell from the way he looks at you. All you have to do is show him that you feel the same way. I swear, Elly, show some sense."

"I know, I know," I said. "I don't want to talk about it anymore right now. Let's just work on the history project."

We did, too, but my mind was on the Luke/Kylee thing the whole time.

7

MARCUS

THE MORNING OF THE FIRST DAY OF SCHOOL STARTED OFF great, but in the afternoon, I had a horrible shock happen—one I'm still sorting out. In English A.P. first period, Ms. Roche taught us how to curse and insult people in Shakespearean English. "Would thou wert clean enough to spit on" was my favorite. I think I'm going to enjoy reading about Macbeth and that awful wife of his. In government class, Mr. Martin let us pick our partners for research topics, so Luke and I teamed up like last year. Then Martin had sort of a lottery to see which teams would pick first and so on. When it was time for our pick, we chose the "Founding Fathers' Feelings on Slavery." Well, it was mostly me deciding on that topic, as I guess I've become more than a little obsessed about learning more about black history after reading those museum letters back in the summer.

Mr. Martin gave us time in class to get started, so Luke and I got out our school-issued laptops and started googling. I know historians say Thomas Jefferson was a great man in so many ways, but I just don't see how he could have written "all men are created equal," while owning hundreds of slaves during his life. He also wrote about slavery as being "degrading submissions" for the blacks and causing whites to become "despotic" and having an "unhappy influence on the manners" of them. With all that high talk, Jefferson did absolutely nothing to stop the practice.

Luke and I learned that even when Jefferson died, his slaves weren't freed. They were sold to other whites and continued on in their lives of misery. At least George Washington had a will that freed his slaves when he and his wife Martha died.

Luke told me something interesting while we were starting on our research. He said the whole rich plantation owner and slave system was very bad for his ancestors. He said that when he researched his family tree in tenth grade for an English project, he learned that his ancestors spent generation after generation in poverty because of the feudalistic system that existed in much of the country then. Too bad, Luke said, that the poor whites and the slaves never got together to complain about how they were being treated. That pairing could have changed history.

Everything that happened in the morning meant nothing compared to what happened after school. Camila wasn't at school today. Early in the day, she texted me and said she was sick and wouldn't be at school. I asked if I could come over and visit her if she wasn't too sick.

"I'm not at home," she said, and I could tell she was crying.

"Well, where are you, if you're not at home and sick," I said. "You're not sick and in the hospital, are you?"

"No, Marcus, I'm not in the hospital, and I was lying when I said I was sick this morning. I'm not at home, either. I'm not even in the same state as you are."

It was then that I got really worried. I could sense the fear in her voice.

"And while I'm confessing to the lies I've told you, I'm also not from the Dominican Republic like I've told you and everybody else. I was born in this country, but my mom is an illegal immigrant from Honduras. The man who I introduced to you as my father is my mother's brother. I've never met my real father; he left my mother when she was pregnant with me.

"That's how my mother and uncle ended up here. They had no job or money. There's so much poverty and violence in

Honduras that they decided to risk their lives coming to America. Mama has always told me that they had nothing to lose when they came here. Her parents had been killed—she would never say how or why.

"On the way to America, Mama was raped several times, once by one of the coyotes that was taking her across the border. Mama and her brother slept out in the desert many nights. Sometimes they would spend a day or more traveling; sometimes they would spend much of the day hiding. Once, they were spending the night in a shack with a different coyote.

"Somebody knocked on the door in the middle of the night, and my mother and uncle hid. They heard shots and later when things had settled down, they found that the coyote was dead. They left right then and walked all night."

Camila then added that she has an older brother, plus a sister who lives with the brother and his wife. Every month, her mother sends some money home to Honduras and saves as much as she can with the hope that one day they could send for other family members or at least one of them. Meanwhile, her one hope was that she could find a better life for her and her family here, and they did, until last night.

Camila said that was when the immigration people showed up at their house, asking a lot of questions and asking for proof of citizenship, which neither her mom nor her uncle has. Finally, after the ICE people left, her mother and uncle talked for a long time and decided to flee and go somewhere else out of state and far away from here.

Then Camila said, "I'm sorry, Marcus. I can't tell you where we're going because we don't know, yet. I doubt if I'll ever see you again."

And just like that she hung up. Camila was out of my life. I've never felt so devastated and depressed.

8

MIA

I KNEW I WAS GOING TO GET A CALL FROM MARCUS TODAY about Camila—it was perfectly understandable and I understood and sympathized with his pain. I've known since I was a freshman that Camila's story about being from the Dominican Republic couldn't have been true. When I would ask her questions about the capital Santo Domingo or why Dominicans are so crazy about baseball, simple things like that, she just gave vague answers.

Finally one day, I said that for someone from the Dominican Republic and who is as smart as you are, you sure don't know much about your home country. It was then that she broke down and cried and confessed that her family was here illegally. She said she had made up the lie about being from the Dominican Republic because it had a more "respectable" reputation than her family's home country of Honduras does.

I understood the lies and the stereotype about certain people from certain Hispanic countries. After all, aren't all Mexicans in this country supposed to be rapists and murderers, just waiting to steal whatever is not nailed down? The Dominican Republic is regarded as a "second world" country instead of a third world one like Honduras, so in the minds of many Americans and in the way many Hispanics think, being from the Dominican Republic would be more respectable than being from Honduras.

Mama and my father argued about many things, especially when their marriage was falling apart last year. But one thing they never argued about was their fierce pride in having a Mexican heritage. And they insisted that my sisters and I should be proud of being Mexican Americans and should be aware of the many good things about our family's home country. I really believe my work ethic came from all those talks about how I should be proud of who I am and where I came from—that I had an obligation to show the world that I am somebody.

The first questions that Marcus asked me were did I know about Camila's secret and if so when had I learned about it? I gave him an honest answer to those questions, and I also answered honestly about if I knew where Camila and her family were going.

"She didn't tell me where she was going," I said. "And if she had started to tell me, I would have told her not to. If ICE knocks on our door and starts asking questions about Camila and her family and where they went, I want to be able to answer honestly that I don't know."

I guess my family and I have been lucky about never having to fear immigration officials. We have all the necessary "papers" and would be glad to show them to anyone. I can't imagine the fear that Camila—and I told that to Marcus—has had to live with all these years. She has a legal right to live in this country; after all she was born here. But I understand the fear that she shared with me, that if her mama and uncle were deported, she would have the choice of either going with them or being put in limbo somewhere. She doesn't have any family in this country that she knows of. She's almost 18, so she can't go into foster care. What "true-blue, full-blooded American" is going to want an 18-year-old young Hispanic woman in their home? Actually, now that I think about it, I would have asked Mama if Camila could have lived with us. I know she would have said yes. But I also understand how Camila wouldn't have wanted to have been separated from her mother and uncle.

After Marcus and I talked over the phone about Camila's disappearance, he had one last question. "She really did care about me, didn't she?" he asked. His words were spoken almost like a whispered prayer and he seemed so desperately wanting me to say that she did indeed care for him deeply. I could tell that he was softly sobbing.

"Yes, she did," I told him, and that definitely was the truth. "When we would go on walks, especially over the summer, she would rave about how you were such a good match for her. Of course, she didn't feel that way when you were a freshman, and you two briefly dated. I remember this time she called you 'a little snot.' But you definitely were very important in her life. I'm so sorry, Marcus. We've both lost somebody close to us."

Marcus and I talked a little more, but we both had said everything we had on our minds. And we both had lots of schoolwork to do. After we hung up, I realized that we had been talking for over an hour, and I had barely started on my college or high school homework. I decided to start on the PSY 230 stuff first and do the reading on "the development of the person's physical, cognitive, and psychosocial growth" from a lifespan perspective, which made me think all over again about the whole Camila mess.

If one of my best friends had been taken away from me when I was a ninth-grader, I would have cried just like I did as a senior. But I feel like I'm better at handling tragedy and disappointment now than when I was a freshman. I think most seniors are. For sure, part of growing up is learning coping skills. Sometimes I also think that one of those "coping skills" we develop is the ability to hide our pain better than when we were ninth graders. At least, it seems that way to me. Maybe, also, we just do our crying in private now instead of in public. I didn't finish all my homework until nearly 2:00. I couldn't stop thinking about Camila, and I guess I cried myself to sleep.

DATE NIGHT

9

LUKE

THE PAST TWO FRIDAY NIGHTS, I'VE GONE OUT WITH KYLEE. The first Friday, she fixed dinner for me at her house. The second, I did the same for her at Granddaddy's and my house. It was a little awkward both times. Kylee lives in pretty much a middle-class neighborhood, so her house is much nicer than mine. Her mom was nice and pleasant, but her dad was sort of distant to me. I can understand that. Seeing a guy in blue jeans drive up in a rusted out, old Ford pickup truck that's got a semi-busted up front bumper—courtesy of Granddaddy the last time he drove—for some reason doesn't inspire confidence in a *young man's prospects*. Maybe I'd better ease up on the sarcasm some before it eats me up.

The dinner itself was real nice. Kylee made homemade pizza for us, which was way better than getting it from some fast food place. She also had fixed some sort of salad and baked an apple pie. I ate a lot of everything. It was really good. We ate down-stairs in the family room and then channel surfed for a while before finally deciding to just talk.

Finally, it was like 10:30, and I said I probably should go home and check on Granddaddy. I had told her about his mental issues. Then it was time for the required kiss, and I just felt uncomfortable about doing that. Kylee is somebody I've known since middle school; she's pretty, she's smart, she's got a great personality, but I don't know...I've just never been interested in her as a girlfriend. There's no... you know... magic.

I think she sensed that I didn't know how to make "an exit," so I said, "How about me paying you back for having me over by cooking dinner for you next Friday at my house?" She smiled and said yes at that, so I took that as my cue to leave.

My dinner was a disaster. I had planned to cook deer tenderloin for us, but when I went rummaging through the freezer all that was left from the three deer I killed last year were some packs of burger and roasts. Thursday night, I got out some roast to thaw in the fridge, but then I realized in the morning that if I put it in the slow cooker during school, it would cook too long and get tough. For sure, Granddaddy couldn't be trusted to turn the pot off and later put the meat in the fridge.

So what I decided to do Friday when I got home from school was put the meat in the slow cooker and turn it up to high. But I didn't put enough water in the pot or maybe it cooked too fast. Because right before Kylee got there, I smelled smoke coming from the kitchen. In fact when she rang the bell, I had just opened the windows in the kitchen to let the stink out.

Kylee saw the smoke and smelled the burnt meat and immediately started teasing me about my "culinary skills." I was glad that she could do that, because I was pretty upset about my screwing up. Then Granddaddy had an accident with his adult diaper, and I had to excuse myself for ten minutes to deal with that. More romantic moments at the old homestead.

When I got back to the dining room, Kylee had made some peanut butter and jelly sandwiches. There wasn't much else in the house. I hadn't had time to go grocery shopping all week with schoolwork and cross country. We paired the sandwiches with the baked potatoes I had made—at least I had been able to turn on the oven to bake them at 400 for 50 minutes—so that was dinner. I had planned to make homemade vanilla pudding but forgot to do that Thursday night after Granddaddy had another one of his spells.

Afterwards, she suggested that we go walking, which was a good idea. I thought about holding her hand but didn't. We made small talk for a little while, and then she said, "There's no special something happening between us, is there?" Then she laughed.

"Nope," I said and laughed, too. "Maybe, the timing's not right. I don't know."

After that, we just walked and talked for about an hour. The pressure was off, and we knew that was the last of our dates. I actually felt more comfortable with her then. I think she felt the same. We talked about English and *Macbeth*, U.S. Government, and the projects we're doing—just random school stuff.

We next talked about what we wanted to major in during college, what we wanted to do for a career—she's now thinking about working for a human service agency —what kind of life we want to have, and what kind of person we want to have as the "one" in our lives.

Right before she left, Kylee really surprised me. "I don't want this to sound weird, but since this is our last date, I know some-body who would be perfect for you," she said.

Remembering that awful blind date with Mary when I was a junior, I said, "I don't do blind dates... bad history with them."

"I'm not talking about a blind date, stupid," she said. "I'm talking about why you should ask out somebody you already know and who's got it bad for you... Elly."

"Elly's not interested in me," I said. "I asked her out twice last year. You probably didn't know that."

"Luke, you're clueless about girls like most guys," she said. "Girls know all of our friends' business. We know who asks who out. Who everybody goes out with and who everybody likes and wants to go out with. I know that Elly knew we were going out. And I know she wasn't happy about it, even though she didn't say so. I could tell by the expression on her face when I brought the subject up one time."

Kylee then added that if I didn't ask Elly out this year, I would always regret it later in life. I didn't want to argue with her, but I'm not going to let Elly shoot me down a third time. I just sort of shrugged and that's basically how our second and last date ended.

10

ELLY

WELL, A NEW GUY ENTERED MY LIFE THIS WEEK—CHRIS, A guy in English class whose family transferred to this area over the summer. Honestly, I had barely even noticed him in class. I guess that's another way I've changed. When I was younger, a new guy transferring into my classes would have been the subject of much discussion between me and my friends. We would have obsessed over every little detail: his looks, what he said in class, and his personality. Now, I just don't care. My dating life has just been so... the word *awful* doesn't even begin to describe it.

So when Chris asked me out Tuesday after class, I was pretty shocked. I hadn't had any dates in months and hadn't felt deprived about the situation. I stuttered around for a little bit, trying to think of a nice way to say "I'm not interested" or "I'm seriously damaged goods, you don't want to even be sitting near me." Or say the real reason I didn't want to go out with him: "I'm sorry, we can't go out because I've got this serious crush on another guy in our class, but I've rejected him over and over and I'm just hoping he'll give me another chance. And I'm trying to get up my courage to ask him out since he probably won't ask me out again. So please don't complicate my life any more than it already is. Thank you, goodbye."

But as has been the case my entire high school dating history, I did the wrong thing and finally said, "Okay," and then one of those long, stupid pauses in the conversation took place.

"*Okay*, as in yes you'll go out with me or *okay* as in you're waiting to know more about what I had in mind for the date?" he asked.

Which made me think the answer was neither of those possibilities. What I wanted to say back was "Okay, as in I'm not interested in you or any other guy besides one right now, and I'm so messed up about that, that I can't think straight about you or any other male." But, no, not good old me, I said, "Okay, as in whatever you want to do."

Chris said we would go to a movie, that we could decide later in the week which one. Oh, great! Stupid Elly can go to a movie with a guy she barely knows and won't get to know any better because they'll be sitting in a dark room for two hours and not talking. Meanwhile, I'll be obsessing about Kylee being out with Luke and hoping, really, really hoping, that their second date is a first-class disaster.

Chris came to our door around 6:30 with my dad answering the door. He always insisted that he get the door and have a few minutes with the "new guy" before we go out, that he wants to "read" the guy first. I'm sick of that act, too. Dad was so high on Caleb and constantly sang his praises, and we all know how that wonderful relationship turned out. I'm so thankful that daddy dearest was so approving of a guy that physically and emotionally abused me the whole time we were the *perfect couple*.

I was in such a foul mood about the whole date that my dressing up consisted of putting on a clean pair of jeans and a bulky sweater. My finishing touches were putting my hair in a ponytail and deciding not to wear any makeup. Mom even noticed my lack of effort when I passed her going down the stairs to the living room. She said, "Elly, when are you going to get ready? He's here." My response was one of those eye rolls that females give to each other. "Oh, my," she said. "I'm sorry. Well, I guess you'll be home pretty early, then."

"You betcha," I said.

And the evening was bad... no worse... than I feared it would be. It turns out that good old Chris is a serious gamer. He had to tell me all about (and I mean *all*) the fascinating, absolutely amazing, awe-inducing, historically important story of how he had made a "fantastic, unbelievable," and those were his exact words, series of triumphs in some computer game he is obsessed about. That story went on the whole time we were driving to the mall to see the movie.

As I recall, my responses to his never-ending story as he droned on and on were, "Oh, my." "Isn't that something!" "Well, wow." Those responses seemed to encourage him to elaborate even more, which served the dual benefit of me not having to do much talking—or thinking—on the way there.

Actually, the car ride was the highlight of the night. The movie was one of those "guy buddy movies." You know, two true-blue friends join forces to wreak mayhem and kill bad guys and then, ultimately, make the world safe for truth and justice, so that ladies can safely walk the streets of this great country again. The two female co-stars were two airheads with short skirts, long bleached blond hair, and lots of cleavage, who, like, had to be saved 50,000 times in the movie by their male heroes. I kept rooting for the two bimbos to die, but no such luck.

When we got back to my house, I was out of the car practically before it stopped... didn't feel like giving game boy a good-night kiss. "Thanks, I had a wonderful time," I said. I started to add "See you in English, next week," but, I thought, why bother to prolong this evening any longer.

When I got to my room, I checked for texts and saw one from Paige. It basically read that Kylee had texted her and said that she and Luke got along just fine on their two dates, but they're not going out anymore. It wouldn't have mattered if they had had a good time. This Friday night, Luke and I are supposed to go cover the football game for Yearbook. I'm going to ask him out on the way home—for sure this time.

11

MARCUS

I HAVE BEEN IN A THINKING MOOD EVER SINCE CAMILA LEFT A month ago. I haven't felt like asking anybody else out for a date. I feel everything is different about me since I was a ninth-grader: my friends, my hopes and fears, what I want to do with my life. How I look at the world. I guess my best guy friend now is Luke, who I used to look down on when we were freshmen. I remember laughing at the jokes and put-downs Caleb would make about Luke being poor white trash. Now, Luke and I often run side by side at cross country practice and work on government projects together.

The other day in school when I asked Luke what he was going to do Saturday, he said he was going to work on schoolwork in the morning, but in the afternoon, he was going to go hiking for hours up in the national forest. He even asked if I wanted to come. So around 2:00, I picked him up and a half hour later, we were at a pull-off at the forest and started running up a mountain. We did that for over an hour, and, man, my body could feel the stress but also the benefits of doing that to get ready for basketball season, let alone cross country.

It didn't take long for my lungs to start burning, but then I got my second wind and just got lost in the experience. Luke

hardly broke a sweat the whole time. About 10 minutes into our
run, he started ragging me and asking if I needed to stop to rest,
that he could carry me back to the car if it was too much for me.
We then both started laughing so hard that we almost did have
to stop.

After we got to the top of some mountain, Luke got out a
water filtering device and said we were going to get some water
from a spring up there and purify it. He said he never liked to
carry stuff, even water bottles, when he was running in the
mountains, that it was just more weight to deal with. It was
really cool to filter that water and drink it. I had never tasted
water like that, it was so...I guess *fresh* really is the word.

On the way down, we talked about a lot of things. He said he
hoped that I wasn't mad about him going out with Kylee twice,
and I told him of course not. Kylee and me were over last year.
He said that she was really nice and all that, but that there was
just no chemistry between them, "as if I know anything about
chemistry," he added.

We laughed at that, too, and then I spilled my guts on how
bad I felt about the whole Camila thing. The dude really listened
to me, which I really appreciated. He said he had had a lot of
bad crap happen in his life, from his parents dying to losing Mia,
to having to deal with his grandfather's mental issues. But now,
he just wanted to concentrate on the future and have a good
senior year...get on with his life. "That's probably what you
should do, too," he said. He's right.

We were about halfway down the mountain when Luke said
he was hungry and said we were going to stop and eat for a while.
I joked that I didn't see any fast-food joints in the woods, and he
said, "There's one right there." He walked over to what he called
a shagbark hickory tree, picked up a handful of nuts under it,
and started cracking them open with a rock he found. Man,
those nuts were good. We ended up sitting there for an hour
eating those things and talking about guy stuff.

By the time we got down the mountain, it was dark, and I
said I needed to stop at the mall and buy some clothes for

school. As things turned out, that was not such a smart move on my part. We were both dressed in sweatpants and hoodies—after all, we had been running—and we were pretty dirty and sweaty. We had gone into this ritzy department store, and I had one shirt under my arm and was reading the label on another one when this mall cop guy came up to us and said, "Hold it right there, you two. Put the clothes down; let me see some identification."

I started arguing with the guy, and the next thing I know, he's calling on his walky-talky for "backup," and a couple seconds later, we're surrounded by four or five mall cops. Twenty minutes later, we're sitting in the store's office, having to explain to two real cops why we were in the store. One of them then asks Luke what his name is and the cop comes back with one of these are you the son of... meaning Luke's dead father... apparently the cop had had run-ins with the man.

Then it was time for Luke to get mad. He said, "Are you arresting me for being the son of a SOB? Are you arresting Marcus for the crime of shopping while black and wearing a hoodie?"

I could tell he was choosing his words real careful when he said next, "I haven't touched a single piece of clothes since I've been in here. All Marcus was doing was looking at two shirts. Search us. We've got nothing on us."

I think it was then that the cop finally realized that all we were was just two dirty, sweaty teenagers in a department store, not two criminals plundering and pillaging their way through the place. The guy even apologized to us, saying that the mall cops had gone off the deep end over this whole thing. That we were "free to go."

We were both pretty shook up while we were walking out of the store. We just kept our heads down, not wanting to attract the attention of anybody. When we got to my car, Luke said, "I'm sick and tired of people comparing me to my father." Then he told me the story of the first time his dad was arrested when Luke was seven. I talked about how last year my dad had given me the "black father's talk," about how a black boy should act if he is ever pulled over or questioned by police. I shouldn't have argued with that mall cop, I said.

"Ain't it great to be a teen on the town," said Luke.

"Yeah," I said. The rest of the way home we made up fake social media posts about what we experienced. My favorite was "Hooded poor white trash kid and hooded black boy terrorize mall by going shopping. Women no longer safe to walk the streets."

We thought about stopping somewhere to get something to eat. But then we thought it would probably be best just to go home and "lay low until the heat was off," as Luke sarcastically put it.

12

MIA

Tuesday of this week, Mama told Isabella, Emma, and me that Friday we were all going to have a "date night" at Sai's house, if that was okay with everyone. Of course, it was okay; my sisters and me have been really curious about that house. Mama's been acting like a teenager; it's "Sai is so great" all the time with her. It's really weird having a mom that is dating. She has a better social life than I do. She spends more time with her makeup to look good before she goes to work at the hospital than I do before going to school. If things keep going where they seem to be going, we all could be living at Sai's house one day.

Also, I've become more and more bored about going out with Mateo. So since he almost always asks me out on Wednesdays, I would have a great excuse, instead of a lame one, why I couldn't go out with him this weekend—that I had to go to my Mama's boyfriend's house on Friday and catch up on schoolwork all day Saturday and Sunday.

Sai pulled up in a brand-new Subaru Forester, a car that's a lot nicer than ours but not like a Mercedes or something that I figured that he would have if he had just bought a new car. Maybe he was just saving money. But wow, that house wasn't something that he and his ex-wife scrimped on. As soon as we got there, he took us on a tour. There's a pool in the backyard, the rooms are all huge, and there's three regular bedrooms for guests and the master bedroom, which is bigger than our living room.

Emma embarrassed me when she said, "Who cleans all these rooms?" Sai laughed and said he has a cleaning service who sends someone once a week, and there's a cook that he has come in to prepare meals for special occasions, like our meal that night. We dined on roast lamb shanks with this honey glaze and had chocolate crème puffs for dessert. Sai and Mama had some sort of expensive-looking wine with their meal. It was so obvious they are into each other. All during dinner, he was making jokes and she was laughing at all of them. No, not laughing, my mama was giggling, giggling like a middle schooler. It was really, really weird for my sisters and me to be there. We were actually watching our Mama out on a date and seeing her acting like she was in love.

You know, I think she is in love. Later after we got home, my two younger sisters came into my room and were full of questions. "Do you think Mama is going to marry Sai?" "Are you okay with that?" "We really like him, do you?" "You know those two guest bedrooms with those big closets, those could be our rooms. Do you want that other bedroom down the hall?"

That went on for almost a half hour before I told them I had to get back to studying and for them to go to bed, that enough was enough. Still, I was glad they came in. Really, I had basically the same questions that they did that I wanted answers for. Yes, I think Mama is going to marry Sai. Yes, I'm okay with that. Yes, I do like him. And yes, I would want that other bedroom down the hall.

I also thought a lot about how all our lives would change if Mama married Sai and we moved into his house. Because for sure, he wouldn't be coming to live in our little house. If they got married before I graduated, I'd probably have my own car to drive to college. This constant stress my family has about money would be gone. We all could have nicer clothes to wear.

How would all that change us? I know this new lifestyle

wouldn't change me. But would it change my sisters? I've seen how some people at school who are well-off act, people like Caleb and Mary. They act...*entitled*, yeah, that's the word. It's just simply *perfect* that those two have been a couple all semester. Caleb can cheat on her and Mary can do the same to him and neither one cares because they think they're getting away with something. They can do anything they want in life. They can raid their parents' expensive liquor collection and come wasted to school like I've seen them come several times this year. And no teacher had better ever give them a bad grade on some test or paper, or they're going to have their parents call and complain about how unfair life is to their sweet babies.

I shouldn't complain about rich people. I know lots of people at school who are well-off and really good people—great friends like Elly and Paige and even Marcus, since he grew up. Still, I'm glad I've known what it's like to be poor and really struggle and see my parents struggle through life. I think it will make me—and my sisters—better people in their adult lives. But I'm not going to mind living in that house, maybe even having a car, if it comes to that.

HOMECOMING WEEKEND

13

LUKE

As usual, Ms. Hawk asked Elly and me to cover the Homecoming game for Yearbook with me conducting interviews and Elly taking pictures of the game, cheerleaders doing their thing, people at the game...that sort of stuff. Since I drove the last time we covered a sport, she said she would pick me up this time.

From the time she picked me up, I could tell something was up with her. She seemed all messed up in the head. I tried to make small talk about how her classes were going, how her brothers were doing in middle school... not much of a response from her at all. Then I asked if she was going to the Homecoming dance Saturday night. That seemed to set her off.

"I've been to the Homecoming dance every year with guys I didn't really care about," she snapped. "I'm done with that."

"I'm sorry," she added. "I didn't mean to talk to you like that." Then there was this long, long pause and she finally continued. "There's this one great, perfect guy I really like, and I want more than anything for him to ask me out, to give me a chance, but I've treated him bad, and I'm really scared that I've blown it with him. I just think we could have something special, and I've been trying to work up my courage to tell him how I feel about him."

"Well, why don't you just tell him how you feel," I said. "I've never understood why you girls just don't come right out and tell guys how you feel about them."

"Maybe it's because you guys are too clueless to pick up on how we feel," she said. "The boy is you, Luke. I've been trying to show you all year that I've changed...that I'm not the airhead about guys that I've always been."

Then it was time for me to have a long pause before saying anything. All those feelings I've had for her came swelling up in my gut. "I didn't know," I stuttered. "I thought... I asked you out twice last year and you said no."

"Well, I was stupid and wrong, and I've realized that for months," Elly said.

"Pull over, we gotta talk," I said.

And she did, and we did talk for the next half hour or so. We both forgot all about the game. I told her I've had a thing for her since middle school, and she said she knew that. But her parents, especially her dad, looked down on me and always had hammered into her that she should date a certain kind of guy.

"Like Caleb," I said.

"Yeah, like Caleb," she said. "And we all know how wise their advice was about him."

"Elly, I want to go out with you in the worst possible way," I said. "But I'm not going to drive over to your house and put up with your daddy's angry looks and crap. And you know he'd be doing everything in his power to keep us apart. He'd be on you all the time about me."

"I've been thinking a lot about that, too," she said. "There's only one solution. We'd have to date in secret. Nobody at school could know, either."

"I'm down with that," I said. "You're right."

"Awesome," she said. "So whatcha doing tomorrow."

"I was floating the river tomorrow in my canoe," I said. "The water's getting colder, but the bass are still active. I want to get in one more trip before it's not safe to float anymore...before winter comes on."

"Then our first date will be going fishing in a boat," Elly said. "I'll make us a great picnic lunch. You have no idea how good I can cook."

"You don't know the first thing about bass fishing," I said. "You have no idea how to paddle a canoe. There are rapids all over that river."

"Then I'll depend on you to teach me how to fish," she said. "You can show me how to paddle through rapids and all that. Aren't you men supposed to keep your women safe?"

She smiled when she said that, and I did, too. Then we realized how long we had been sitting there, and if we didn't hustle, we were going to miss the kickoff. I didn't want to have to explain to Ms. Hawk that we missed part of the game because Elly and I were making plans to go out on our first date.

The whole game was like a fog. All I could think of was being alone with Elly and showing her how much I love the outdoors and how to make good casts and paddle through rough spots in the river. To sit beside her on a riverbank and talk and eat. I would have been happy—no, thrilled—to go anywhere with her. But to do something with her in the outdoors was like a dream, especially since she is not really, by a long shot, an outdoorsy girl.

When the game was over and we were walking back to the car, I wanted to hold her hand for the first time. When we got back to the car, she said, "I wanted you to hold my hand back there, but I knew you couldn't in public with our 'rule.' Tomorrow?"

"Tomorrow," I said. "Meet me tomorrow at my house at 1:00. I can get Granddaddy fed and have something prepared for his dinner. I think he'll be okay by himself."

Then I told her what kind of clothes to wear (warm clothes and no cotton ones because they absorb water like crazy if a canoe turns over), and I emphasized that she should bring a change of clothes in case we did have an accident.

"Well, then, boy," she said. "You'd better keep me safe."

"You can count on me," I said. I would never let anything bad happen to her.

14

ELLY

I FINALLY GOT ENOUGH NERVE TO ASK LUKE OUT WHILE WE were on the way to cover the Homecoming game. I was hoping he would say yes—and he did—but I wasn't sure after the way I've treated him. To my surprise, I didn't even mind that our first date was going fishing in a boat. I just wanted to prove to him that I had changed and I cared about the things that he cared about and wanted to get to know him better.

The first thing we did was something Luke called a shuttle, where we parked my car at the take-out and then drove to the put-in with his canoe. Before we started, we sat in the boat on the bank, and he had me practice making all these types of padding strokes: draw right, draw left, forward and reverse strokes, J-stroke...that sort of stuff. I was really confused by all that, and as things turned out, I so much wish now that I had told him I didn't understand everything he was talking about. Then he showed me how to cast, and he put his hands on my arms to position them right. It was just wonderful—the patience and tenderness he showed me. I'm not used to guys acting like that.

But my not telling him about my confusion on the paddling thing wasn't the only way I screwed up. I forgot that he told me not to wear cotton, so I had on a pair of jeans and a cotton blouse and just this flimsy little jacket that I wore because I felt like it would make me look really good for him. I spent so much time on my makeup and hair that I almost forgot to bring the change of clothes that Luke told me to bring. I didn't charge my phone, which turned out to be another mistake I made. All I brought was another pair of jeans and another cotton shirt. I admit I was a little distracted because I had lied to Mom where I'd be—that I was going over to Mia's house to hang out with some other girls.

The first part of our date went just great. I caught my first ever fish, what Luke called a smallmouth bass. I wanted to take a selfie of me, Luke, and the fish, but then I realized who was I going to show the picture to as Luke and me both feel that we should keep this dating thing secret. We went through a bunch of what Luke called easy Class I rapids, and everything was going great. He caught some really big fish. He was identifying these birds by the way they sang, and we were talking nonstop. I was just so glad to finally be alone with him.

Then it happened. We were about halfway through the trip, and there was this big rapid coming up—Luke called it a Class II —and he said we would be fine "going through it." I just had to do what he told me to do when he told me to do it. The closer we got to the rapid, the bigger those rocks looked; the faster the current was flowing, the more scared I got. We were partway through the rapid, and Luke told me to draw left, and I froze up and did nothing.

The next thing I knew, we hit one of those rocks, the boat overturned, and both Luke and me were pitched out into that cold water. It's a good thing Luke had insisted that we both wear life jackets or I don't know what would have happened. I went under the water, swallowing some of it, and then I screamed when I came up for air. I guess I panicked... well, I did panic. I was so cold when that water hit my chest.

All of a sudden, Luke grabbed me around the chest with his

right arm and shouted out, "I've got you; just hang on to my arm. It's okay. I'll swim us over to the bank. Trust me."

I just went limp. I was so cold I couldn't have done anything, anyway. The next thing I knew, Luke's pulled me up on the bank and kept asking me if I was okay. I was shivering so hard I couldn't stop. Then Luke shouted that the dry bag (our dinner, extra clothes, and this stuff of his were in it) had come loose and was floating free from the canoe. It was then that I realized that I hadn't "strapped in" the dry bag behind me like Luke had told me to. I decided it was the wrong time to admit that little error.

It was a good thing I hadn't secured the bag because things would have turned out worse if I had. Luke ran down the bank for a little ways, then jumped back into that cold river, and swam after the dry bag. Meanwhile, the overturned canoe just kept getting further and further away and then went out of sight. A couple minutes later, Luke got back to me.

"You're going to be okay," he said. "I'm going to start a fire with the matches in the dry bag. Take off your wet clothes and put on your dry ones. You'll be warm before you know it."

He then walked over to me and gave me a hug, and I hugged him so hard back, and then it finally hit me what had happened. Panic just washed over me, and I couldn't stop crying and shaking. He held me even closer. Once I finally started to calm down, I looked into his eyes, and we kissed for the first time.

"I'm so sorry, Luke. I shouldn't have frozen up," I said.

"It's okay," he said again. "Let's just get you warm."

He never complained about how I had screwed up, never complained about how cold he was. I could see that he was shivering hard too, but he wouldn't let on about it. I kept thinking about how other guys I've dated would have handled the situation. Caleb and most of the rest of them would have been screaming and cursing at me for me causing the whole accident. All Luke was concerned about was warming me up and making sure I was okay. A few minutes later, he had this roaring fire started. Luke arranged our wet clothes around the fire so they could dry out. When he got out my lightweight shirt and jeans, he just sighed and then he did the sweetest thing—he gave me his warm jacket. I had caused the accident. I hadn't helped fix things. I hadn't strapped the dry bag in. I hadn't brought the right kind of clothes, so he gave me his. All I had done was sit there in the boat and panicked. And he never brought any of that up.

Then he said, "We're halfway through an eight-mile float. It'll be dark in a couple of hours. There's a mountain behind us and a mountain ahead of us that we'd have to climb no matter whether we went upstream or down. We're cold, tired, and stressed out and could get lost in the dark. I've got to find my canoe, too. It's old and beat up but I can't afford to lose it. Elly, I'm sorry, but we've got to spend the night here."

15

MARCUS

I HADN'T BEEN TO A FRIDAY NIGHT FOOTBALL GAME ALL YEAR. I miss everything about those games: the smell of the grass, the anticipation, the roar of the crowd when we run out on the field, being with my teammates, and most of all I miss the competition. But I know if I got another concussion, it could mess me up for the rest of my life. I just couldn't stand sitting up in the stands and watching some other wide receiver play my position and be constantly thinking whether I would have beaten the other team's cornerback on a play.

But my brother and his longtime girlfriend Jordan came home from college for the weekend, and Joshua insisted that the two of us should go to the Homecoming game. Joshua and Jordan have been dating since their sophomore year in high school, so I guess it's sort of a permanent relationship. Later, I found out just how permanent it is. When I told Joshua I didn't want to go, he said he had asked Coach Dell if we could sit on the sidelines with the team. Joshua started at tight end all four years he played, and him and Coach Dell are tight. That it would be good for both of us to be around the guys again.

It wasn't good for me. The first quarter, this huge linebacker rang the bell of one of our wide receivers when he ran a slant across the middle. The guy is just a sophomore and had to be helped off the field. Early in the second quarter, one of our defensive backs got carted off the field when his leg got pinned up under him in a pileup. It looked like a torn ACL to me—the same injury I had. I couldn't take seeing those two guys in pain; it was too raw—too much like my injuries. Finally, I told Joshua that he could stay but I was calling Dad to come pick me up.

Joshua could tell that I was suffering inside; he's always been real good about reading me. So he said he would leave with me, but instead of going home, he said let's go to the country club and shoot hoops. He could feed me the ball and let me practice making jump shots. I was down with that with basketball season coming up.

We ended up doing as much talking as practicing. My brother told me that he and Jordan had decided to get married when they graduated from college. That they weren't going to tell their respective parents yet, but he wanted me to be the first in the family to know. I wasn't surprised at the news. I'm glad she's the one for him. He then asked about the whole Camila thing, and I told him I was just now getting over it a little bit, but I had to move on. "That's healthy," he said.

Next, I told him about Luke's and my run-in with the cops, and Joshua then asked if Dad had told me the "new, green Honda Accord story" where our father got pulled over by the police when he was driving while black. I said yeah, last year, and my brother said that Accord was one of many reasons why Dad gave me an old piece of junk to drive when I was a sophomore. That I had been so immature then that I would have run my mouth if some officer had pulled me over and who knows what would have happened then. That I had much less of a chance being pulled over while driving a junk car than a new one.

"You know, Marcus, some punishments Dad gave us—some of the things he did like giving you an old car instead of newer one—probably didn't make sense to you and me when we were younger, but I think he always did try to do his best by us," he said. "I think he's been better than a pretty good dad."

"Yeah, you're right," I said. "That old car, the lectures, the 'you've got to work for things' talks. That always be respectful, be courteous to others, and don't embarrass your family stuff. Those sayings of his all seem pretty wise now, but they sure didn't when I was a freshman and sophomore."

"How about you telling the old man that the next time you two are alone?" he said. "Bet he'd appreciate that."

"I will," I said.

"One more thing, little brother, I think you should start checking out the girls again," Joshua said. "Now, that's something I thought I'd never say to you. One of your kid problems was that you were too obsessed with them. But I think it would be good if you were at least in the talking stage with a girl or two."

"Maybe, I will," I said. "Wouldn't hurt."

Parents, girls, sports, cars, we had pretty much exhausted guy conversation topics. The last hour we were at the club, he just fed me the ball for jump shot after jump shot. During one stretch, I hit eight treys in a row. Most of the night I was right on and zeroed in. Of course, it's easy to sink bombs when no one is guarding you in an empty gym at 10 at night. Still, my form felt good. I told Joshua that, and he agreed I was silky smooth.

On the way home, he asked me if there were many girls at school that would be awesome girlfriends for me. I thought about girls like Kylee that I had dated and ones like Amber, Mia, Hannah, and Leigh that I hadn't —girls that maybe I should consider. I don't know what I'm going to do about the dating thing. I do know that it was real nice to spend the night talking with my brother. Sure know I wouldn't have thought that when I was a kid.

16

MIA

Earlier in the week, I finally made up my mind about calling Luke, so I did. At first, he acted like he seemed surprised to hear from me, which is understandable. I mean, I hadn't talked to him for a long time, and we don't have any classes together. I felt a little lame asking how his classes were going. Predictably, he's struggling in Statistics and Spanish...no surprise there.

I asked him if he was in need of a tutor, which made him laugh and made me hope that somewhere inside him there were still these hidden feelings for me. "I really appreciate all those times in ninth and tenth grade when you tutored me in the library," he said. "The talks we had, the things we did together."

He didn't add, but he could have added, "until your father broke us up and you did nothing about it... you didn't want to date secretly." There was a long pause, which was so awkward, because there never used to be long pauses in our conversations. We always had so much to talk about.

Finally, I asked—and again I seemed so lame—if he would like to get together this weekend either Saturday or Sunday. Luke said he was busy cleaning the house and taking care of his grand-daddy Saturday morning—that his granddaddy's "mental issues" were a major burden, and with school and cross country so time consuming during the week, he had to spend most of every Saturday morning cleaning up their place, grocery shopping, and paying bills. Then I asked him if he was free Saturday afternoon, but he said he was going to be "out in the outdoors" all that afternoon, so I assumed he was either fishing or going deer hunting then.

"How about then sometime Sunday?" I asked, and he replied again that his grandfather's care took up much of the morning with bathing him and other things, plus he had some studying to do. But I could come over around 12:30 after lunch, and we could go for a walk. I was so thrilled when he suggested that; maybe there is some hope for us to get back together? Do I want that? Does he deep down want that, too? If I don't want that, why am I wanting to talk to him? All I definitely do know is I've got to absolutely know how I feel about him. Years from now, I don't want to be filled with regrets about what could have been.

About two hours before I came over, I got this weird call from Elly's mother. She wanted to know if Elly had woken up yet and how was the girl talk at the sleepover? Also, if Elly were awake, to have her call if it was convenient. I stammered around for a little while before I realized if I kept that up for long, Elly's mom would get suspicious. Obviously, Elly wasn't at my house, there had been no sleepover, and there was no going to see if she were still asleep.

Elly is one of my best friends, maybe even my best one, and I didn't want to be the one that got her into trouble with her mom. Not long ago, Elly told me that she used to lie to her mom all the time when she was younger, but she was through doing that, that she wanted to justify the confidence her mom has for her ... that she was all through with that behavior. What's changed that would cause her to start lying again?

Finally, I said that all of "us girls" had stayed up really, really late, and I was still the only one up. I was sure that Elly would call her first thing when she woke up and came upstairs, but if she hadn't called, I would make sure that she did when I first saw her. The lies just puked out of my mouth. As soon as I said bye to her mom, I texted Elly immediately. About ten minutes later, there was still no answer so I called her—no answer. I didn't know what to do, but I knew what not to do—answer my phone if Elly's mom's number came up on it.

Eventually, it was time to walk to Luke's house, but when I got to his house Sunday afternoon, nobody answered when I knocked on the door. It was unlocked so I walked on in. I figured Luke might be in the back taking care of his grandfather. I walked down the hall a little ways, and I found his granddaddy sitting on the floor and moaning and there was this awful smell. It was clear Luke wasn't there, and this is gross to say, his grandfather had pissed himself and worse.

The man didn't recognize me, which was understandable even though I had been around him quite a bit when Luke and I were dating. It's been two years since he saw me and his mind has gone downhill a lot since then.

I thought the right thing to do was to clean up his grandfather and give him something to eat, because the one thing he kept saying was "I'm hungry, I'm hungry." It took me a good 20 minutes to sponge bathe him and find him some clean clothes and underwear to dress him with. There wasn't much in the fridge except some frozen peas and broccoli, and I found some potatoes in the larder, so I cooked up all that along with some deer burgers that I found in the freezer.

It was nearly 1:30 before I finished all that. I had been so busy with taking care of Luke's granddaddy that the thought never occurred to me that Luke would never have willingly left the man alone like that unless something had happened. Had something awful happened to Luke while he was out in the woods or on the river?

HOMECOMING WEEKEND CONTINUED

17

LUKE

I was so mad at myself when Elly and I overturned our canoe on our first date. I thought she seemed confused when I was explaining the paddling strokes. I should have made sure she knew what those paddling terms meant. When I told her to draw left (which means placing the paddle parallel to a canoe and "drawing" the paddle toward the boat), she didn't know what to do. Anyway, the canoe overturned when we hit the rocks. We were lucky that the dry bag's strap had come undone and I got the bag back, or the worst could have happened. We could have died from hypothermia without dry clothes to put on. No way would I have been able to start a fire because the matches would have been in the dry bag floating down the river inside the canoe.

So I was able to get a fire going really quick. We put on dry clothes from the dry bag, and I gave Elly my jacket to help her warm up faster. I was still really worried that she was going to get hypothermia. I broke off dead branches from trees, stuck them into the ground near the fire, and arranged our wet clothes on them. It was then that I realized that I just couldn't afford to lose my canoe, and it would be way past sundown before we could walk to either one of our cars. So I told Elly we were going to have to spend the night there. I was afraid she was going to get real worried or real mad when I said that, but she said, "I trust you. Do what's best. I really mean that, Luke."

So I went to work preparing for the night. I took my Buck knife out of the dry bag—I carry that knife every time I go anywhere outdoors—and went to look for some small pine trees. I found some back in the woods and cut off lots of branches and made several trips back to our camp, carrying them. I told Elly that we were going to sleep around the campfire, and I was going to make things as warm as possible.

Next, I used my knife to cut off four five-foot or so limbs from small trees. I then shoved two limbs, at an angle, into the ground around the fire. I always put trash bags in my canoe, so I can pick up crap along the river that slobs have left there. I tied the first trash bag to the limbs and made a lean-to for Elly. Then I put the empty dry bag under the lean-to for her to sleep on top of so she wouldn't be lying flat on the ground and get so cold overnight. I piled up some of the boughs on the two ends of the lean-to for insulation. I left the side facing the fire open so the heat from the fire could get to her. I told her to use her lifejacket as a pillow. That would get her head off the ground, too.

Then I made my lean-to the same way as Elly's, except there was no dry bag for me to sleep on. So I cut up lots of little pine boughs to put under my lean-to, so that I could have a little insulation from the ground. I knew it was going to get down in the mid to upper 30s that night. I could sense it in the way night was coming on. Then I spent the rest of the time before sunset bringing every little scrap of dry wood I could find back to our camp.

If I could wake up every hour or so all night, I could keep the fire going until sunup. I figured the cold would wake me up real often anyway, so it wasn't like I was going to get much sleep. The last thing I did was take my water filter and its quart container and go to the river and purify enough water to get us through the night and the next morning. Just before dark, I finished everything up. I was relieved to see that Elly had stopped shivering.

She had taken our meal out of the insulated tote bag in the dry bag and had warmed over the fire the chicken salad and deviled eggs she had made at home. I was absolutely exhausted from the whole ordeal, but at least all that work I had done making sure we were set for the night had made me not so cold.

"Luke, I've been watching you the whole time," she said when I sat down beside her. "Thanks for taking care of me."

"I just wanted you to be okay and not be so cold," I said. Then we looked at each other, and I knew more than anything that I wanted to hold her tight and kiss her, and I did.

It would be stretching things to say that we had a long, romantic dinner. We were both so hungry that we gobbled down our dinner in like three minutes. We both wanted right then to eat the four apricot Clif bars I had put in the dry bag as emergency food, but I finally decided that we had better save those for breakfast. It was then that I realized that her parents were going to be worried about her. Thank goodness I had told her to put her cell phone in the dry bag before we shoved off.

"I texted Mom and said I was going to have a sleepover at a friend's house," she said when I asked if she had contacted her parents. "I promised myself that I wasn't going to lie to her anymore. But if I had told her the truth, Dad would have probably tried to have gotten the National Guard to come rescue me."

We laughed at her joke of her dad leading the National Guard on a rescue mission into "the wilderness." For sure, he would have freaked out when he saw that I was the one she was out in the middle of nowhere with. Then I piled a lot of wood on the fire, and we went to sleep.

18

ELLY

WHEN LUKE TOLD ME WE HAD TO SPEND THE NIGHT ON THE riverbank, the first thing I knew I had to do was text Mom and tell her that I wasn't coming home that night. The first lie I thought of was that I had decided to spend the night at Mia's house with friends, so that's what I texted. My phone was almost dead when I did that, and by the time I remembered I had better let Mia also know about my "sleepover," in case Mom called about something, it was dead. I was furious with myself for not charging it up before I left home. One more screwup by yours truly.

I got even madder at myself because I just sat by the fire shivering. I just couldn't get warm. Meanwhile, Luke was off gathering wood and making me a place to sleep by the fire. The only helping I did was place our food next to the fire so it could warm up a little. Obviously, chicken salad and deviled eggs are things people usually eat cold, but I don't think either one of us wanted to eat anything cold. I wish we could have stayed up late and talked and watched the fire glowing in the dark. It would have been so romantic, but we were both too exhausted after our "little ordeal" as he kept calling it. All night long, I would wake up every little bit because I got cold, but the next thing I would know, Luke had gotten up to put more wood by the fire, or I would wake up and he was watching the fire to make sure it was going good. Once I woke up, and I could see his flashlight off in the woods, and a little while later he was back with more wood.

When morning came, I was really glad he had insisted that we save those four Clif Bars for our breakfast. I was so hungry that I could've eaten all four of them. He's such a great guy that he probably would have let me if I had asked him to give them to me. I made up my mind right then that I was going to do something really great for him on our next date, if there is one. No, I knew even right there on the riverbank that there would be a next date with him. The way he took care of me all night. He does really care for me even with all my flaws.

After we "broke camp," as he called it, we headed for the river to walk along the shoreline so we could try to find his canoe. Luke said it would take about four to five hours of steady walking "to get out of here" and to my car if we didn't find his boat. But it would take much less time if we found his boat—and even less time if we found the paddles.

We had been walking along the bank for about 20 minutes, when we found one of the paddles in what Luke called an "eddy." He had to strip down to his underwear and wade out up to his waist to get the paddle back. Well, he saw me with practically nothing on last night when I had to strip off my wet clothes. There's no "mystery" now about what we look like without much clothes on. Daddy dearest would have freaked out about that, too.

About an hour later, thank God, we found the canoe too. We both started yelling with like sheer joy when we first spotted the boat. It was hung up in some brush next to the bank and once again Luke had to strip off and wade out a little bit to get something. Of course, he paddled us out. Even if he had found the other paddle, I don't think he would have trusted me with it to help him. You know, Luke never mentioned that because of me, he had lost both his fishing rods and all the "tackle," as he called it earlier, that he had brought. I know how little money he and his granddaddy have. Just one more thing for me to feel guilty about.

When we got to my car, I was so relieved that as soon as we got out of the boat, I practically ran over to him and gave him the biggest hug I could and kissed him.

"Are you going to kiss me like this every time I almost drown you?" he joked.

"Luke, you know this whole thing was my fault," I said. "You're just not saying it."

"I just wanted to keep you safe," he said. "This was a really bad idea for a first date. That's my fault, not yours. We should have gone hiking or something and had a picnic—gone anyplace on land instead of taking you out on a river in October. It was stupid of me."

"Well, how about our second date being going hiking and having a picnic next Saturday?" I asked. As soon as I said that, I wished I hadn't. Boys should always make the first move. My mom has always hammered that into me, but then I was glad when I asked him out, even though it was me that had asked him out for our first date, too. I'm sick and tired of all those stupid rules about what girls should do and shouldn't do. I wanted a second date with him, and I said so. So what!

And I was super glad when he said right back, "What's for lunch and what time do you want to meet?"

We had to hide his canoe in the brush while we did what Luke called "the reverse shuttle." I drove my car to the put-in, and then we hopped in his truck and drove back to the take-out where we loaded his canoe onto the truck and drove back to get my car. I had been with him straight for almost 24 hours, and it was like the best 24 hours of my whole life, no matter all the stuff we had gone through.

When we said goodbye at the put-in, we kissed and hugged each other again for the longest time. When I was on the way home, it was then I remembered that I was going to have to go back to good old lyin' Elly, one last time—hopefully the last time, that is. What kind of lies was I going to have to make up for Mia and my mom?

19

MARCUS

Saturday afternoon after I finally finished all that schoolwork I had to do, I decided to go to the mall and buy those clothes that I was supposed to have bought that time Luke and me almost got arrested for "shopping while dressed as teenagers wearing hoodies." This time, I was dressed more *respectable*—jeans and a shirt tucked in. I bought and paid for— can you tell my sarcasm—the shirts I picked up on my way out. Then I decided to stop at the mall's coffee shop to get something to drink.

While I was in line, I saw Hannah sitting over in a corner, reading her government book. Then I remembered Joshua's and my talk from the night before, about my needing to maybe get my mind off Camila and start dating again. So I thought why not, I'll buy some coffee, go over and see if she invites me to sit down, and just see if karma exists. She was, after all, one of the girls I mentioned to my brother that I considered date-worthy.

Well, I did go over to Hannah, she did invite me to sit down, and we did have a great time talking. The government project she was working on was American laws designed to keep out minorities. She was researching how the United States worked a whole lot during the 1800s to keep Chinese out of the country, the "Yellow Horde Peril" and all that. She was really into it. I told her about my research back in the summer on prejudice against blacks during the twentieth century wars, and before you knew it, we were engaged in this deep conversation about how things are today with prejudice toward people like her who are Hispanic and, obviously, toward people like me.

We got so into all that, that we must have talked about the topic for over an hour before we finally slowed down—it was intense. I mean, this girl was something else, so I thought, why not ask her out...it's karma that we met up like this. She got this strange look when I asked her, then she hesitated for what seemed like a long time, and finally she said.

"Marcus, I'm gay. I'm not out. I keep it hidden because my parents, especially my dad, would freak out if he knew. He'd probably sign me up for 'conversion therapy' with some quack PhD."

I stuttered around for a while and finally said, "I've seen you with other guys since we've been in high school."

"Marcus, those guys are beards," she said. "You know, where someone goes out with someone else just to get out of the house or to help a friend out. Some of those guys were gay, too, and just wanted to reassure their parents that they were straight by going out with a female. It's all very convenient for everybody. It keeps me from being called a *faggot* in school or from having those little snarky phrases like 'that's so gay' or 'she's so gay' directed at me."

For the next hour or so, we talked about her being gay and that was real interesting, too. She had known since she was in middle school that she preferred girls, and she was worried about her parents and peers rejecting her, not to mention her Catholic church. Though, she said, maybe her church should have been more concerned about the rumors that their priest was a pedophile and preying on little boys instead of "whether a 17-year-old gay Hispanic girl was a mortal threat to the church." From talking to her, it was apparent that I wasn't the only high school senior at the mall in a sarcastic mood.

Finally, I asked her how many people at school knew about her secret and when and if she was going to tell her parents. Hannah said that Mia, Elly, Paige, and Kylee knew for sure, and there were probably some others that strongly suspected but didn't want to say anything.

"My parents split up when I was a ninth grader," she said. "I've always worried that their arguing over me and 'the way that I was' was why they got divorced. I live with my mom. My dad lives nearby, and I see him every other weekend. I've actually fantasized about texting Mom and telling her that I'm gay, but maybe a text is not the best way for her to find that out."

Hannah laughed when she said that but then grew serious and said, "I'm trusting you, Marcus, by telling you all this. I still don't want to come out."

"I respect that," I said. There was silence for a while, and then I finally said.

"Let's go out anyway this Friday night. We can be the other person's hot new thing for the night. I can tell my brother I'm back in the dating game. You can tell your mom what a great time you had with this stud guy."

That Friday night, we actually did go out. I paid for her meal, and she paid for mine. We had a great time. There was absolutely no pressure—no worrying about first date nerves, no worrying about whether or not to give her a kiss, and no worrying about a second date. Early on, we both decided that it would be both our first and last "date." She updated me on how her Yellow Horde research was going, and I told her about how I was going to be a walk-on for the university's basketball team next year. I mean, it was a nice evening.

When I was driving Hannah home, she said she had some suggestions for some girls that I could ask out. "You know Kylee still talks a lot about you," she said. "And Mia thinks you're pretty cute, too."

"Kylee and I have already tried the dating thing two different times," I said, "and she broke up with me both times. Mia is on, like, this whole different plane from everybody else at school with her being so smart and wanting to be a doctor and all that. She's a little intimidating."

"Sometimes, even us smart girls can use a night out with a smart guy," she said.

"Maybe so," I said. It was something to think about.

20

MIA

AROUND 1:45, LUKE FINALLY GOT BACK TO HIS HOUSE, AND HE looked just awful—his clothes were filthy, his hair all matted down, and he had this huge rubber bag slung over his back.

"Oh, Mia, oh no, you've been waiting for me. I'm so sorry," he said. "It's been awful. My canoe overturned, and I had spent the night on the river."

Then he told me what had happened, how his canoe had hit a rock and then overturned, how the dry bag broke free from the boat, losing his fishing gear, having to build a fire to get warm, finding the boat the next day and paddling out...just now getting home.

"Luke, you should never have gone canoe fishing by yourself," I said. "You used to tell me all the time how unsafe that was."

I wanted to add that if he ever needed a second person for one of his canoe trips, I might be available to go, but did I want that? Well, why was I there if I didn't want that. I don't know what exactly I want from him. All I know is I've got to spend some time talking to him before senior year is over to see if there is still something between us that is precious and good and wonderful—things that I couldn't stand to be without no matter what or how many miles and states were between us.

"Granddaddy!" he suddenly said. "Where's Granddaddy? Is he alright?" I took Luke into the living room to show him his granddaddy was okay, and it was then that he must have heard the washing machine running.

"You did laundry, too, didn't you?" he said. "You had to clean him up, too, I bet? Mia, how can I ever thank you. You're so wonderful. I swear. Thanks so much."

Then he gave me a hug, not one of those long, tight, intense hugs that we used to share, but just a quick one—a friend-type hug. What was I expecting anyway? How can I be so in control of my thoughts and emotions around other students and adults, be the so-called "smartest girl" in the school, and be the stereotypical "woman on the rise"? Yet this boy makes my brain turn to mush. Well, what's wrong with that? We did have a special relationship for almost two whole years. He is a great guy, and I'm a special young woman with a great future. Maybe that future could still include him; maybe we could be a couple again—this time permanently. I've got to know one way or the other.

"My mom's a nurse," I finally said, and it sounded so lame. "I know how to take care of people."

"Thank you so much," he said again. "I'm flat worn out. I had to keep a fire going all night I was so cold. I haven't had any sleep since Friday night. I've still got to get the canoe off the truck, do more laundry, and... crap, I forgot all about my Spanish test for Monday and my U.S. Government project. Mia, I'm sorry. I can't go on a walk with you today or even spend time talking."

I would have helped him with all those things, especially the Spanish stuff because I used to do that all the time, but he didn't ask for my help, and I didn't want to intrude. He was obviously exhausted. I was thinking what to say when I just blurted out, "Maybe, I could come over next Saturday afternoon and we could have our walk and talk?"

He got this weird look on his face when I said that and he said, "Come over at noon next Sunday for lunch. That's how I can repay you for all you've done. We can go walking after I get Granddaddy fed and down for his afternoon nap."

I told him that would be great and then it was time for me to leave. It was probably good that we didn't have time to have a long talk. Maybe by next Sunday, I'll have my thoughts and feelings for him better sorted out.

When I got home, I checked my phone and had all kinds of texts. One of them stood out, especially the one from Hannah. It said, "I've just told another person I'm gay. Call me."

Obviously, that had to be text number one. Probably better than anyone, I know Hannah's long struggle with the gay thing. When we were ninth graders and the subject of boys would come up—like it did nearly every day at lunch—she often seemed indifferent to the whole guy thing. I didn't really think anything about that then. When we all became sophomores, and Camilla and I and a lot of our other friends, especially my Hispanic ones, were finally allowed to date, Hannah said her parents were still forbidding it. I thought that was really strange and awfully harsh of her parents, but now I know it was just a convenient lie, her saying that.

Hannah finally confided in me when we were juniors that she was gay but made me promise that I wouldn't tell anybody. That her parents would freak out if they knew and haul her off to the confessional booth at church. I remember one time trying to make a joke about her going to see our priest during confession and him telling her that he was gay, too. That he then said he knew someone who was just right for her, but she didn't think that was very funny.

I think Elly, Paige, Kylee, and Camila—well, Camila's gone—are the only ones at school who know Hannah is gay, and I'm probably the only one that knows she's been secretly dating this junior girl at our school. Why do I have to be the one other girls tell their deepest secrets, too? I can't believe ICE hasn't come to my house yet and asked about Camila. Maybe there are too many Camilas all over the country to chase down?

The last big reveal from Hannah was that Marcus and her

had decided to go out on Friday night as strictly friends, and she had already told him that she was gay. She said she didn't want to lie to him. Good for her. She also said that Marcus was awfully cute and smart and had really grown up a lot. "Maybe you should be the one that goes out with him," she said.

I don't know about that. I'm having enough trouble right now sorting out my feelings for Luke.

A MONTH LATER

21

LUKE

ELLY AND I HAVE BEEN DATING A MONTH NOW AND everything's been awesome between us. I always thought and hoped if she ever gave me a chance, she would like me—that we would be good together. We're still keeping our thing secret. On our second date, we drove separately to the national forest access road and we spent the day hiking in the mountains and having a picnic lunch. I teased her about finally dressing right because she showed up wearing a polypro pullover and fleece pants. She's not ever going to be an outdoors girl, but the fact that she wants to spend time out in nature with me means everything to me.

That's why for our third date, I suggested she come over on Saturday night to my house, and we could cook dinner together. Elly was real thrilled with that suggestion and said that she would go to the grocery store right before she came and bring everything she needed. She said I could help with the cooking, but she wanted to do all the deciding on what we were going to have. That meant a lot to me, too.

Once we had decided what we were doing to do for our date, the next thing was figuring out how to "smuggle" her into the house. She obviously couldn't drive up to my house and bring in a bag of groceries. I finally came up with the idea of her driving up to the woodlot that runs behind the houses in my neighborhood. She could park at a lot that hasn't been built on, and I would meet her in the dark where the woodlot begins. We could walk through the woods until we got to my backyard. I'm glad it's November and it gets dark so much earlier now.

She fixed some kind of chicken dish, I don't remember the name of it...it doesn't really matter. It tasted great, and I was with her—that's all that matters. I do remember that she baked an apple pie for dessert. I hadn't had a dessert with a meal in a long time. When I get home from school and have to take care of granddaddy and sometimes clean him up, I'm too tired to do much with dinner, except thawing out or warming up something.

I'm also glad that cross country season is over. I mean I really enjoyed it, but the meets and the practices took up a lot of time. I finished third in the regionals in the 5-K, which I was really proud of, especially since I haven't been doing competition running for as long as a lot of the people I went up against.

The best thing that cross country has done for me, besides helping me get in real good shape, is that it helped me get into the local college. Yep, I've got a partial scholarship, based on academic need and with the "stipulation" that I run cross country for the college, too. The admissions office wasn't real happy about my grades—how could they be with my 2.4 average —but they said there were "extenuating circumstances" with my "situation." That I had potential. Me telling them I want to be a teacher probably helped things a lot, too. Mrs. Whitney said there's not a whole lot of people lining up to be teachers these days because of the low salaries. I've never had any money so having a schoolteacher check one day is bound to be an improvement over what I got mowing lawns when I was a kid and working as a janitor.

School has been going pretty much as expected. I've actually got an *A* in both English and U.S. Government, the usual *C*s in most of the other classes, and the usual *D* in both Statistics and Spanish. Actually, I'm doing worse in Spanish than math. It's usually the other way around. The other day Ms. Lewis gave us this test on Spanish homonyms. It was a disaster from the get-go.

Granddaddy had a bad night the night before the test, which didn't help things. He has this rattling cough that won't go away, and he keeps having accidents during the night. He wakes up and comes into my room, and I have to go clean him up or I hear him coughing all night and have to go in and keep checking on him and giving him cough medicine or something. So I didn't get hardly any sleep the night before the test.

The homonym test started out with *hambre*, *hombre*, and *hombro*. One of them means *man*. Another means shoulder or arm or something and the last one means you're hungry. I got so mixed up that I missed all three of those answers. Then came *casar* and *cazar*. One of them has to do with marrying; the other has to do with hunting. I was so tired I couldn't remember which was which. Then I thought that Julius Caesar was this great leader and great in battles, so I went with *casar* as the word meaning to hunt. I didn't remember until I had turned the test in that Caesar was a Roman dude not a Spanish one.

So I got those two questions wrong, too. Ms. Lewis just sighed and shook her head when she gave my *F* back the next day. At least, I made her laugh—I mean she and the whole class couldn't keep from laughing—when that same day I pronounced *la comida* as *la chlamydia*. I guess it's good for a class to have one real stupid person in it—somebody around for "comic relief" as they say. I won't be majoring in Spanish or math in college. That's for sure.

22

ELLY

So much has happened in the last month. This past Friday, Luke and I had our fourth date. We sort of schemed together to have it. The basketball team had its first game of the season on Friday night at Lewis, so we told Ms. Hawk wouldn't it be neat for us to cover an important away game for the Yearbook. Luke and I could do sidebars on students who traveled to the game, interview the players on what it was like to try to overcome a crowd cheering against our players, and, maybe, hopefully, write about how a big road win "made" the season. Ms. Hawk said sure as long as my parents and Luke's granddaddy gave us signed permission to go.

Obviously, Luke's granddaddy didn't know what he was signing, but my Dad sure did. He wanted to know why we just couldn't ride the bus with the basketball team, and I said it was because we'd have to leave earlier and get back home later because of "all the logistics and postgame stuff." Dad sort of bought all that, but then he began lecturing me about being "careful" around Luke and not doing anything to "encourage" him. He said he was going to buy me some pepper spray for me to keep in my purse—"just in case Luke got out of line."

What Luke and I really wanted to do was to go out for

dinner some place where nobody would recognize us. We went online and found this really nice steak and seafood restaurant not far from the school where the game was to be played—but a good two hours from our school. I knew Luke was going to be worried about the cost for the dinner. I didn't want to embarrass him by offering to pay for it, so when we looked over the menu online, we decided then to order the least expensive meal— flounder almondine—and not have any dessert or even get coffee.

It was the first date we've had out in public, and it was so wonderful to go out with him at night like that. I had to be careful how to dress because I didn't want Mom to be suspicious on why I was wearing some really cute outfit for a basketball game. Luke doesn't really have nice clothes to wear, so I didn't want to overdress anyway.

We have so much to talk about all the time, and it was no different on the drive down there and back and at the restaurant. He wants to know how I think about things like politics and religion, the environment, social issues...just everything. We agree on just about everything, but more importantly than all that, when we don't agree, he doesn't put me down. I'm not used to a guy treating me like that.

Already, I'm having strong feelings for Luke, but I know from all my past screwups with guys that I need to take things slow. This month, I got officially accepted to the local state college, so now Luke and I are going to the same college. Dad and Mom have said repeatedly I could live on campus if I wanted to, but I've finally decided that I'm just going to commute. It's only a 12-minute drive.

There are other reasons I decided to live at home. I don't want to be around all those temptations that have always fouled me up before. The drinking, the parties, and the likely chance that drugs will be at some party. I feel like I'm strong enough now not to do something stupid like I've done in the past, but still, it's better for me not to be around that drama.

When I told Luke about my deciding to live at home, I was

so hoping that he'd say something like, "Great, we can maybe carpool," and you know what, he did! He actually said that. I really do think we'll be together next fall. My mind started spinning about us always being together. Why do us girls, as soon as we're with somebody for a few weeks or a month, start thinking about how things could be way in the future? Slow down, Elly. But, still, he is really special and different.

I've had my mind so much on Luke, school, and college that I finally remembered that I had never apologized to Mia last month for texting Mom that I was spending the night at her house when Luke and I got stranded out on the river. Mia and Paige are probably my best friends, and I don't want to lie to either one of them, but I just had to lie in this case.

So the day before Luke and I were to go out to dinner, I called Mia and said I was so sorry for taking so long to apologize for involving her in the sleepover lie. Mia and I haven't had a chance to talk much this year because her morning college classes have caused us not to be together in any of my classes at school. We caught up on school-type talk, and then Mia said, "Can I ask where you really were that night?"

I hadn't planned on her asking that and my mind had been on Luke and me, so the first lie that popped into my head was a whopper. "I had a date with a guy over at the local college, and I ended up spending the night at a dorm with this girl I know from church. I was afraid my parents would freak out about the whole college guy-dorm thing." I mean that's a pretty involved lie on short notice. I'm surprised that even I came up with something that good. I'm not proud of that; I'm really ashamed of myself, but what else could I have done?

Mia then said that she was thinking about having a "real" sleepover at her house this Saturday night. She wanted to talk to me about some things. Since Luke and I were going out to dinner on Friday, I said sure. Does she want to talk about getting back together with Luke? Inviting him over to her house or something? I don't want Luke to go over to her house, but can I say that to him? I don't want to try to control his life, either. I want him to really feel that I'm what's best for him. He's been the only boy that I've ever thought I might actually have a future with.

23

MARCUS

I'M ABSOLUTELY THRILLED THAT BASKETBALL SEASON FINALLY started Friday night. Running cross country was fine, but there's like ten people watching when you compete in a meet, and that's nothing compared to the atmosphere at a football or basketball game. Coach Henson and I talked a lot about what position I should play my senior year. I knew I was going to be a starter, but Coach didn't feel that I had the explosiveness anymore to be shooting guard. A torn ACL will do that to you, and I didn't think my body could take the pounding of those bigger guys if I played small forward.

With Quentin graduating last spring, the solution was obvious. Coach Henson and I finally decided point guard was the role for me. I'm taller than all the other points in our region; maybe some of them out-quick me but not by much. And I'm better than a decent dribbler and I'm a really good passer from those years as a shooting guard.

Before the game started, Luke and Elly came over to me and Luke interviewed me for a Yearbook story while Elly took close-ups of me. Luke asked some pretty good questions, like how was I planning to show senior leadership to the younger guys, how hard was it going to be to play the point, and what were my predictions for the season as far as the final standings and possibly making regionals? You know, I think there's something up with those two or something's about to be up. They sit next to each other in English and government. I've seen them walking in the hall together. The way she was sort of leaning in to him when they walked up to me. Maybe I'll ask Luke about that.

I had a turnover right off the tap. The other team's power forward went in for a slam and the crowd went nuts. Then Lewis' shooting guard drained a three, and with less than a minute being played, we were already down five, so my career as the "floor general" was not off to a particularly sweet start.

I admit I was a little stunned at the start, but then I heard Coach Henson yell my name, but not in a bad way. He yelled "Marcus," like to catch my attention, nodded his head yes, and like mouthed the words "You got this" and nodded again. Then he flashed the hand signals for me to run the give and go with our sophomore center Garrison. This is his first year on varsity, but I mean the guy is a stud and has got these really sure hands and sweet moves.

I passed the ball to Garrison in the post, broke for the basket, got the ball back, and slammed that sucker down, hanging on the rim just a little to let Lewis know that we've got ball, too. Then it was their turn to have a turnover. I got the ball back and got it down low to Garrison again, and he posterized Lewis' center on an up and under scoop shot. He faked that guy right out of his shoes.

After they missed a long three—that was a really stupid shot —we got the ball back. They were expecting me to feed Garrison again. Instead I faked a pass in to the post, their small forward collapsed into the middle, and then I hit Coby, our sophomore shooting guard, for a wide-open trey. We never trailed again the rest of the night.

Yeah, the game was tight all night, but I felt like we were in control – I was in control, the rest of the night after Coby's three. We ended up winning by six points and Garrison got 17 and Coby 15. I only got 10, but, man, I think I had one of my best, my most complete games ever. I went two of four from the field, six of six from the line—all in the last two minutes when Lewis was trying to foul me so that I would miss free throws and they could catch up. No such luck, suckers. With an eight-point lead, I'm glad to be fouled and drain free throw after free throw and let you fools make two-pointers. Meanwhile that old clock was ticking down to double zero.

But what I was most proud of was my 11 assists, three steals, and only two turnovers. Right after the game in the locker room in front of everybody, Coach Henson bragged and bragged on me for my leadership and overall floor game. He said it was the best game I've ever played. I swear, it was. After that first minute, I felt like I was in control of the whole flow of the game.

I feel good about everything right now, except not having a girlfriend. I really miss that. Twice, Hannah and I've gone out and done some things together, but, obviously, those have been Plus One situations—you know the kind of relationship where you're just friends and you're going somewhere together just to have someone to go with. Hannah says her mom thinks that I'm her first boyfriend, which Hannah thinks is so funny. She says her mom has always not so secretly thought she was gay, and now her mom believes Hannah has "finally seen the light" and has "a man in her life."

On one of our "dates," Hannah had me over for dinner, and her mom was just gushing about how great I was for her daughter. I'm glad to help her out, and I enjoy her company and conversation, but I really want a real girlfriend.

24

MIA

I'VE TRIED TO LIVE MY FOUR YEARS IN HIGH SCHOOL LIKE THE perfect person, the perfect student, the perfect friend—the A-plus-100 percent in everything person. Early on, my parents put a lot of pressure on me to be that way, and I put a lot of pressure on myself, too. It's hard to say whether they put the most pressure on me or I did.

Now that I'm older and supposedly wiser as that old saying goes, I don't feel so perfect anymore. Yeah, I'm going to be the valedictorian of my class, and I've got a full scholarship to the best university in the state. Yeah, everybody in school knows who I am, and I'm *the* role model for all the ninth and tenth grade Hispanic kids. That's nice. That's great, in fact. I can live up to being a role model. But I still have hopes and fears like everybody else, and I need reassurance from my friends and from Mama. I can forget about getting that from my father. It's almost been six weeks since my sisters or me have heard from him. Well, that's his problem, not mine, anymore.

All those things are why I had my best friends over for a sleepover last Saturday night. I wanted to be silly for a few hours, eat junk food, stay up late, gossip, and talk about guys and school rumors. None of the things I do when I'm doing my perfect role model performance at school and at college. I also wanted to have a night where I wasn't studying way past midnight in my perfect role model starring role.

Things got off to a great start. Conveniently, Mama and my sisters left to have a dinner and movie night at Sai's. Elly and Paige brought the pizza, Kylee and Hannah brought diet sodas, and Leigh joined our little group. She brought several cartons of mint chocolate chip ice cream. I don't know why we bothered with diet sodas, the way we stuffed ourselves for about an hour.

Then the big reveals started to happen. Hannah said she had finally convinced her mama that she wasn't "a lesbian that was going to rot in hell," thanks to Marcus being her Plus One. They had already planned how they were going to "break up." Hannah said she was going to tell her mama that she had caught Marcus kissing another girl in school and that he "had broken her heart." She was going to become so *crushed* that she "didn't have the *heart* to date any other guys for the rest of the school year." Then all Hannah had to do was survive her mom's "When are you going to get a boyfriend" questions during the summer, and before you knew it, she'd be off for college where she could finally have a girlfriend out in the open—hopefully, she said.

Paige's big reveal was that she and Allen had been arguing a lot for the first time since they started dating in ninth grade. Allen's going to the university and plans to become a lawyer and move to some urban area, where there's more opportunity to make money. But Paige is going to the local small college and wants to do social work and live around here. She doesn't want to break up with Allen, but she fears that's what he wants. She doesn't know what to do. None of us knew what to do, either, but I really feel that we helped her some by just listening.

This type of thing went on for hours until around 1:00 when finally everybody had gone off to sleep except Elly and me. I knew she had been wanting to talk to me in private, and she knew I knew that. Finally she said, "I want to apologize to you for getting you involved in the sleepover lie thing I told my mom. I shouldn't have done that, but I was desperate, and I really, really am sorry."

I said I understood, but then she continued.

"I was also lying when I told you I spent the night at a college dorm with a friend from church. I apologize for that, too."

"Where were you then?" I said.

"I'm not going to lie to you ever again, I promise," Elly said. "But I'm not going to tell you where I was that night...not right now, anyway. I'm sorry. I just can't." There was this long pause, and then she added, "It's very personal."

"I understand," I said, but I didn't really. Had she spent the night with a guy? That doesn't sound like Elly. Had she secretly gotten back together with Caleb? That would have been a horrible mistake and I just blurted out all of a sudden that I hoped she hadn't gotten back together with him.

"No way!" she practically shouted. Then we both laughed because she had said it so loud that we were afraid she had woken up everybody. Then it was my turn to reveal something.

"I'm thinking about having Luke over for dinner some night. Before I go away to college, I've just got to see, to know, if we still have feelings for each other. But the times I've called him up, he's been busy with his granddaddy or school or stuff. I was supposed to have gone over his house a couple of Sundays ago but his granddaddy was having those spells of his and Luke had to cancel. I know you work with him a lot in Yearbook and spend a lot of time with him at games and working on spreads and stuff. Do you know if he's dating anybody? Is he interested in anybody? Does he ever mention me?"

She had this long pause and finally said, "Every time he's ever mentioned you, he's always said really nice things about you, how you made this huge difference in his life."

"But do you think I should ask him over for dinner and see if there was still something between us or could be something again between us?" I said.

There was another long pause and she finally said, "I think you should do whatever you think best."

"Then it's settled," I said. "I'm going to do it. Hopefully, he'll be free some weekend soon."

CHRISTMAS COMES BUT ONCE A YEAR

25

LUKE

FOR MONTHS GRANDDADDY HAS BEEN ASKING ME WHEN I WAS going to be 18, and over and over, I kept saying December 10. Sometimes I'd think those were the only times he seemed to be aware of what was going on. But sometimes 20 seconds after I told him when, he'd ask the same old question again. Last week on December 10, he was asking me and finally I was able to tell him that I was 18. He still asked me a half dozen more times if I was really 18. I've always felt that he was worried what would happen to me if he died before I turned 18.

Two days later, I was in Yearbook class, and I got this call from guidance to go see Mrs. Whitney. I was really surprised at that. I'd gotten into a college. She doesn't have to do any more scheduling of classes for me. When I walked inside her office, she told me to shut the door and sit down. It was then that I knew what was coming next. A soon as I sat down, she said, "Luke, I'm so sorry, but I just got a call from your grandfather's daycare center. He's had a stroke. They couldn't resuscitate him. I'm so sorry to be the one to have to tell you."

I had all these emotions rise up in me. He's always been my favorite person, my role model, the person I've loved the most— the person who loved me unconditionally. He took me in when I ran away from home. He didn't have much, but he shared with me everything he had. But he really wasn't Granddaddy anymore and would never be again. To be honest, I've been just worn out trying to take care of him before and after school. I'm going to miss him like crazy, the Granddaddy I once knew, but that guy was gone, and he was suffering all the time and couldn't do any of the things he loved like gardening and talking to me at dinnertime. I told Mrs. Whitney all those things and then I said, "I'm glad he's gone. He's been in awful pain... the coughing, the trouble breathing..."

I know this sounds selfish of me, but deep down, I was relieved that I didn't have to care for him anymore. I hope that doesn't make me a bad person, but I just couldn't go on much longer taking care of him. Mrs. Whitney asked me if I needed to stay in her office and talk some more or just go home, but I said no to both. School was almost over for the day anyway.

When I got back to the room, I sat down next to Elly and got back to work. She could tell I was upset. She said, "Is it your grandfather?" Then she looked at me and saw me fighting back the tears, "Oh, Luke, I'm so sorry. I'll drive you home from school. Let me help you."

"You don't have to do all that," I said.

"Luke, no discussion, I'm doing it. I want to help. You need me."

I do need her even though we've only been dating two months. There have been a lot of great things, but the absolute best thing has been talking to her on the phone before I go to sleep every night. Some of what we talk about is just school stuff. She'll call out my Spanish vocabulary words for me, make up these crazy sentences with the new words, and go over my Statistics homework with me. Obviously, we can't go to the library and have her help me with those things or sit together in the lunchroom. The best kind of talking with her is when all the schoolwork has been finished, and we just talk. You know, hopes and fears, dreams and goals, life after high school, life after college, what kind of teachers we'll be.

When we got home from school that day, she asked me if she could make the funeral arrangements and all that for me. But it was then that I remembered to tell her that Granddaddy had long ago arranged to be cremated because it was so much cheaper. He didn't want any service because of the expense, and I hadn't wanted an urn with his ashes. I have all these wonderful memories of him, I told her. I don't need a container of ashes.

Elly then asked what I wanted to do with his clothes, to keep his room the way he had it for a while longer or what? I decided to clean out everything right then and be done with it. I didn't want to be reminded of those adult diapers anymore, and his clothes were so old and worn out that probably nobody would have wanted them. I told her all that, too. The only thing I wanted to save from him was his old pocket watch, the one his grandfather had given him.

Elly said she would pick out the clothes that maybe Goodwill could use and then put the rest in the trash. So for the next couple of hours, we took care of all of Granddaddy's possessions. When everything was all sorted out, she asked where the vacuum was and she made his room spotless. It was almost 8:00 when we got all that done; actually, she did most of it. We then remembered we hadn't eaten, and she even took care of that, fixing egg sandwiches for both of us with milk. She said that kind of meal would help me sleep better.

After she cleaned up the kitchen, it was 9:00, and then I got worried her parents would be worried about where she had been. She just smiled when I said that and said, "I'll think of something, I always do."

26

ELLY

I KNEW SOMETHING AWFUL HAD HAPPENED TO LUKE'S grandfather when he came back from guidance. I could tell it from the look on his face. I really wanted to help him with the funeral arrangements or anything else that needed to be done— to make it easier on him.

In the past when I would do something nice for a guy, it was all part of trying to get in good with him, not because I was trying to do the right thing or be a good person. With Luke, it's different. I'm trying to do the right thing just because it is the right thing—because, already, I do care for him. He's bringing out the best in me. I just feel different around him, feel better about myself than when I've been with other guys. I want him to feel that I can bring out the best in him, too.

Cleaning out his grandfather's room and fixing Luke's dinner later really made me understand how poor those two were...Luke is. The man's clothes were, like, decades old, and the house was so shabby and dirty. It looked as worn out as those clothes, but the way that Luke speaks with such—respect is the word—about his grandfather shows, and I know this is super lame to say but it's true—that those two guys were rich beyond money.

I didn't get home from there until 9:30, and I'd been so busy that I had forgotten to text my parents about where I'd been. Mom met me at the door, and she was just frantic. I've decided to do my best to try not to lie to her anymore, so when she asked me where I'd been, I said at Luke's.

"What?!" she practically shrieked.

"His grandfather died this afternoon," I said. "I was helping him with getting things in order."

Then my Dad, like he always does, started in on Luke. "You shouldn't have been alone with a boy like that."

"A boy like what, Dad?" I said. "Like Caleb, the boy you and Mom liked so much from our church that was always trying to get me to have sex with him. Caleb, the boy whose dad you had to call because he kept spreading all those lies about me on social media. Or Matthew, another boy you all liked so much who got drunk and caused me to be in a car wreck. You know what, Luke did touch me while I was there. He hugged me for like two seconds when I left. Maybe that was when I should have sprayed him with the pepper spray you gave me. The nerve of that lower-class, low-life boy to touch your little Princess Elly."

I started to stop right there, but I was so wound up, I kept on going.

"We're on Yearbook together. We sit together every day and work on what Ms. Hawk has assigned us to do as editors. We're friends. His grandfather just died, and he needed help. What was I supposed to do when I found out his grandfather died, just keep on working on our spreads like nothing had happened?"

I swear, I've had it with their attitude, especially Dad's, about some things. Sure thing, my Dad came right back with some attitude.

"Just because you're almost 18, little girl, it doesn't mean you've suddenly learned how to be an adult. We didn't know those things about Caleb and Matthew. You should have told us."

Well, maybe Dad had a point about that, but I was so mad and tired from the long day that I was in no mood to admit it. I started to say something smart about how he had been so gushy over Caleb; he would never have listened to me anyway. Instead, I just said I was going to bed and went up to my room.

When I checked my texts, there must have been dozens of them. All from my little group of senior girls, plus Marcus and Allen. They all wanted to do something nice for Luke, go over to his house, and clean it up for him and fix him some meals. Mia had organized the whole thing. It was really a nice gesture on her part. The old Elly would have been jealous of Mia doing that, but, no, I don't want to be that person anymore. I want Luke to see me as the best person for him because I truly am, not because I schemed and conned him into liking me. So I sent out texts saying that I had been over at Luke's house that night helping him get things straight—more honesty on my part—but there was still a lot to be done. Could everybody come over there on Friday night? After another round of texts, we had things set for then.

I was lying in bed when I remembered that I hadn't talked to him before we go to sleep like we always do, but I figured he was asleep by then, and I didn't want to wake him. I wish he had a cell phone. Almost everybody in the school has one. I could have texted him to see if he was still awake.

I was so wound up about everything, especially about arguing with Dad, that I couldn't go to sleep. It's Christmas in two weeks, and I've been wanting to get Luke something. We will have dated two and a half months by then. I know the whole Christmas gifts for guys is one of those things that who knows what the right thing to do is. Like, how long do you date a guy before you give him a Christmas gift?

Well, I don't care about those stupid teenage rules for girls anymore. I played by those rules and all it got me were pathetic, awful boyfriends and binge purging myself until I was sick. You know what I'm going to get Luke—a toaster. The one in his house doesn't work, and I'm going to tell him I bought him one because he needed it.

That way I can buy him something practical, and maybe he won't feel that he has to buy me a real gift. I feel better about myself than I ever have. I've got a great boyfriend, and I'm done lying to my parents and everyone else.

27

MARCUS

One of the best things about the Christmas season is all those Saturday night basketball matchups where we get to play good teams outside of our district. We had our first one last Saturday and another one this weekend. To be honest, I've never played better than I did last Saturday.

The first four games of the season, I've just concentrated on getting my teammates involved. I wasn't looking to shoot very much because that's not the most important thing a point guard has to do. My most important job is to distribute the ball, keep our big men involved and moving, and the defense guessing. For last Saturday's game, we had to take a bus trip three hours down the interstate to play Johnson City. They've got three guys who are going to play Division I hoops next fall. None of those guys are five stars, but they are fours and they've gotten scholarships, so they're studs. Their point guard is one of their four stars.

I guess the guy thought I was some kind of a nobody because he came out playing me loose, or maybe he had watched the tapes and decided that I was only a pass-first type point. I drilled three threes in the first four minutes of the game and fed Coby for two three pointers and Garrison for four baskets in the lane

—all on their home court. We were up 12 at the end of the first quarter against one of the top 10 teams in the whole state.

At the end of the quarter, Coach Henson told us that Johnson City was too good a team not to make a run at us, but when they did, just keep our composure and keep playing hard, especially on defense, and things would eventually turn out okay. Coach was right about the run. They started off the second quarter with an 8-0 run before Coby finally got out on the break and I fed him for a layup.

But then they hung another 8-0 run on us, and the next thing we knew, we were down a bucket, and they kept that two-point lead all the way to halftime. They'd go up by four or six, and we'd come right back, but we could never tie them up. I had two turnovers during that second run and two more before halftime. I was really pissed about my play. Usually, Coach wants to do all the talking during halftime, but he told me this year that if I think the team needed chewing out, that I as a captain should do it, so I did.

I had the guys huddle up in the locker room and I apologized for my four turnovers, but I also said we were too good a team to roll over against Johnson City and let them have a 16-2 spurt. That we had proved how good we could be in the first quarter and this game could make our whole season, and that we could play with anybody in the state if everybody bought in to playing team hoops. Coach Henson didn't say a word the whole time I was talking.

But when he sensed I was done, he said, "Do what Marcus is telling you to do. We can play with these guys. We can outhustle them for loose balls and play in your face defense. Box out on defense and pound the boards on offense. We'll win this game if you guys do that. I promise."

I broke the huddle and looked over at Henson, and he gave me one of those approving nods of his. I could tell by the way he looked at me that he believed in me, that he had trust in me to call the right plays, make the right decisions, take the big shot, make the right pass ... the whole deal. I felt in total control when I went back out on the court.

We made a stop on defense to start the half, and then Garrison bulled his way in for an offensive rebound to tie it up. For the rest of the third quarter, the lead seesawed back and forth like that. We'd be up by two or three, then they'd have a little spurt, then we'd come right back at them.

It was like that into the fourth quarter, too, until there were about two minutes left. We were down one and Johnson City had the ball and was milking the clock. Their point tried to make a pass into the paint, and I deflected it. Garrison picked up the ball and spotted Coby streaking down the court and hit him with a bullet pass. Coby slammed that sucker down, and we were up one.

I think that whole sequence thing unnerved their point guard a little because he seemed to be in too much of a hurry the next time down. I picked his pocket and headed toward our basket, fed a bounce pass to Coby, and again he slammed it. We're up three with less than a minute to go and they called time.

Coach Henson huddled us up and said, "One more stop, guys, just one more stop and it's over." He instructed me and Coby to double-team their point guard when he crossed half court and said that would throw everything off, and it did. Mr. Four Star point got all panicky, probably because he couldn't believe what was happening and he was running out of time. The ball got loose, I picked it up, and Coby and I played keep-away for ten precious seconds with their coach screaming, "Foul 'em, foul 'em!" They finally fouled me, and I drained both free throws, and just like that the game was over. Yeah, they drained a so-what three at the buzzer, but we won by two and that's all that counted.

We celebrated all the way home on the bus. It was the biggest thrill I've ever had in sports. What made it even better was on the way home, Coach Henson told me that two of the assistant coaches at the university had come to watch the game. He hadn't told me they were there because he hadn't wanted to put any more pressure on me. He said that if they weren't impressed with my overall floor game, then they didn't know squat about basketball. I've got to believe they were impressed.

28

MIA

When I heard about Luke's granddaddy dying, I just knew that I had to do something for him, so I texted all the people that he's friends with or I'm close to and asked if they could come over to his house Friday night. I'm so frustrated that I've still not been able to have him over to my house for dinner or go see him at his house. Either he's been busy, or I have, but that's not why I organized everybody to come over to his house. I just wanted him to know that people care about him.

I got there about 4:30, and Elly was already there. My plan was for everybody to bring something for dinner at 6:00 and then leave the leftovers for him to eat in the days to come. One of the reasons I got there so early was so that Luke and I would have had at least a little time to talk for a while...not necessarily about possibly getting back together but just to talk so I could maybe figure out how he felt about me...about us. Honestly, I was pretty disappointed that Elly had beaten me there. She even answered the door.

When Elly opened it, she said Luke was at the kitchen table and they had been working on his homework for Statistics and Spanish. I had brought one of Luke's favorite dishes, chicken enchilada casserole. It was all fixed but needed to be put in the oven to cook. Elly said she would take care of the cooking, that they had finished the stats homework, and maybe I could help Luke with his Spanish?

So I sat down with Luke while Elly went to work in the kitchen. She certainly knew her way around his kitchen. I guess that's understandable since she was over there the other night. Finally she left to go vacuum the living room, and I had some time alone with him.

"Luke, I'm very sorry about your granddaddy," I said. "I know how much he meant to you."

"I really appreciate you saying that," he said. "But I'm okay. Elly came over two nights and Allen and Paige were here one of those nights. It's just that he was really the only person in my family that I was really close to and could talk to. Mom loved me, but Dad...you know how things were with him." Then his voice sort of trailed of.

His right hand was holding a pencil and was on top of the stats book, and without thinking, I just reached over and put my hand on top of his and squeezed it. Just touching him in such a little way caused all these feelings for him to bubble up to the surface, just like in the past. He squeezed my hand back, but then he let go, not holding it for a long time like he used to do.

When I leaned over toward him, I had really wanted him to do the same thing. When I held his hand, deep down I had wanted him to really hold on tight for a long time. But maybe that was unfair of me to expect that. After all, he was grieving for losing the only person in his family he had left. Then he said, "We'd better start working on the Spanish."

We didn't even get to do that long. I heard Elly stop vacuuming, and the doorbell ring, and soon after that Allen and Paige came into the kitchen and started working on the dish the two of them had brought, some kind of soup. Before long, the house was full of people, and I barely got time to talk to Luke the rest of the night.

Right before I went home and when only Marcus and Elly were still there, I asked Luke if I could come over Sunday afternoon and check on him. He seemed hesitant at first, but then said okay. But I didn't even get to keep that date or appointment or whatever you want to call it with him.

When I got home that night, Mama told me that she and Sai wanted to take my sisters and me out to lunch on Sunday and then afterwards go over to his house. Mama seemed really excited, maybe even a little mysterious when she said that. Later that night after my sisters had gone to bed, she came into my room and said she had something to say.

"You know Sai and I have been dating for about six months now, and we've decided to get married in May. I wanted you to know first. I need to know that you're okay with this. I've worked with him for years, and he's such a good man. I'm really lucky that he and I both were in need of somebody at the same time."

I am happy for her, but I was still really disappointed that my latest attempt to be alone with Luke had failed. I mean every time I try to plan something with him, something comes up. Maybe over the Christmas holidays things will work out.

The lunch with Sai went really great. Isabel even screamed out loud at the announcement; she was so excited. When we went over to his house afterwards—soon to be our house, too— which is just amazing considering the types of places we've always lived, I was just as silly as my sisters were when I was picking out my future bedroom. Mama and I then picked out a spot in the backyard where we could raise a garden and another place where we could plant some fruit trees. I wouldn't be surprised that the neighborhood probably has some ordinance where people can't raise chickens—things are a little snobby there. Still, we won't have to worry anymore about having enough money to pay the electric bill and worrying if we can afford to turn on an air conditioner in the summer.

THE MINOR CHARACTERS

29

CALEB

I HATE THIS SCHOOL. I'M SICK OF IT, BEING HERE FOR FOUR years. It's been like a total waste. Every morning when I wake up, I feel like I've got to have something to drink. Not a lot, but just something to start my day off right. I lie in bed until Mom and Dad go off to work and then get into their liquor cabinet and have a shot or two of whatever's in there. It helps me to focus.

Sometimes they mess around and I have to wait an extra-long time for them to leave and it makes me late for first period English 12. That class is a joke anyway. Why should I be in a hurry to get there? It takes Ms. Williams like 15 minutes to get started. By the time she takes roll and half the class comes in late, she has to keep starting over with the boring lesson. She keeps telling people to put their phones away or their music "devices." Nobody listens to her. Why should they?

I probably should just get a bottle out of the closet and keep it in my room. My parents would probably never miss it, but if they did, all I'd get is one of them stupid lectures my old man especially is always giving. They are both so lame with what they call *discipline*.

Like the time Elly's dad called and complained about what I had posted on social media about his sweet, little daughter. I posted she was a slut, and I broke up with her because she kept sleeping around on me. That showed her she can't get away with breaking up with me. She should never have dumped me last year. No girl in her right mind would dump me. She's worse than a slut. She's a fat slut that doesn't know she's a fat slut. Dad kept complaining that he has to work with Elly's dad, and things are a little tense between them anyway since we broke up. I don't care about my old man's problems. He's never done anything for me.

Anyway, every time I get three more tardies, Ms. Williams—she's never going to get a man to look twice at her because of her horse face—writes me up, and I get my choice of before or after school detention. I'm not coming early to school, that's for sure, so I have to go to the detention after school and sit around with all these losers who've got nothing better to do. First-year teachers like Williams act all tough but she's got no clue on how to teach. Who cares about Macbeth and that old lady of his—she's a slut, too. That Old English literature crap is another huge waste of my time. I can't understand a word those people are saying. Williams acts like this is the most important thing that's ever been written—what a pathetic no-life loser.

My grades aren't worth crap. My GPA has gone down to 2.1. The only thing saving me is my grades from ninth and tenth grade. I haven't gotten anything better than a *D* since then. Why bother. Ever since I quit the football team, there hasn't been any reason to study. I'm going to graduate no matter what I make this year. Every time there's a test that I absolutely have to pass, it's easy just to put the notes on my phone and keep it between my legs. The teachers at this school walk around half blind.

Mrs. Whitney has been on my case all fall, and I'm sick of that, too. She says I'm not going to be able to get into the university if my grades don't "dramatically improve." Well, my grades aren't going to "dramatically improve" because I don't care if I don't go to the university. I had planned to be a walk-on there for the football team. Ever since I quit the school's football team my junior year, I figured I'd walk on at the university and sooner or later I'd be their starting quarterback. The guy

they have now isn't worth crap and probably leads the conference in fumbles and interceptions. It wouldn't be saying much to
say that I would do a better job quarterbacking than that no
talent. For sure, Coach Dell made a mistake this year not
begging me to come back to lead the team. I bet he's still regret-
ting it. I was tired of his mouth anyway.

Another thing I'm sick and tired of is Mary. It used to be fun
getting bombed out of my mind with her—throwing back shots
of tequila, getting high over at her house when her parents were
gone, good times, good times—but she's just a slut that gets all
teary-eyed when she gets drunk or stoned. She constantly wants
me to tell her how I love her and is always telling me how much
I mean to her. She's pathetic. She's worse than pathetic; she's
desperately pathetic. I'm gonna drop her as soon as I find
someone better, which won't be long.

Officer Dodd has been on my case, too. Yeah, he's just what
this school needed—another goon with authority issues. He
busted me at Homecoming a couple of years ago and ever since
he's got this "I've got my eye on you" attitude. Like, he's such as
big, tough cop that the police had to take him off vice or something or whatever he was doing and come be the big tough dude
taking care of business here. Yeah, right.

I know he was following me around the other day. I told
Williams that I had to go to the bathroom, and she said no and I
said, "Then, I'll have to take a piss in the trashcan." A couple of
the guys in class laughed out loud. After that little pearl of
wisdom, I just got up and left and Williams didn't say nothing.
Matthew told me later he was going to have to remember that
line and use it the next time he wanted to go.

Williams must have contacted Dodd or something after I
left. I really can't remember too much about that morning
because that was one of my three-shot, liquor closet mornings—
and when I came out of the bathroom, there he was. I got two
days of out-of-school suspension because it was my "third
offense" for "cutting class." I didn't cut; I had to take a piss—
how can they not understand that?

30

HANNAH

I'VE KNOWN I WAS GAY SINCE I WAS IN SIXTH GRADE, BUT back then, I was too scared to say anything to anybody. Now all these years later, I'm still not all the way out. I don't see that changing while I'm at this school.

Earlier this month at Mia's sleepover, I came out to Leigh, so that makes five with Elly, Paige, and Kylee already knowing, and of course, Mia has long known. I'm not expecting me being gay to be "celebrated," by them or anybody else. I'm very thankful that my best friends have accepted me for who I am. What I'd like is just to have a girlfriend out in the open, someone I could go on dates with, to proms and homecomings with, to walk down the hall holding hands with. I don't think that's asking too much. To just have a healthy relationship with somebody, that's all I want.

I think, I know, that a lot of kids are okay with gay people at the school who have come out. I've read those news stories online about what used to happen to gay kids at schools and in society, so I know things are better today, and friends like Mia and Elly keep telling me that to make me feel better. But things aren't as good as they could be...should be.

My Mom is never going to understand or accept who I am. I know that. She's all about how our Catholic church calls it a sin, but then she so conveniently ignores all the scandals about homosexuality from the pope's office on down. Those are just stories, she says, and they're probably not really all true and just exaggerated. It's not that bad in the church, she keeps saying. Actually, I think it's probably worse than what people think, than what she thinks. I've seen how our parish priest acts around little boys. He's creepy, but Mom thinks he is so Godly and a "gift from above." That he's normal—and I'm not. So, no, I'm not coming out to her.

I felt so smart when Marcus and I were conning Mom about our "red-hot" relationship. At least, she was off my back for a while about her mission for me to "be dating nice, high school boys." I don't feel bad about deceiving her. She had it coming, the things she's said over the years, the fears that she expressed about my sexuality, the times she tried to set me up with boys from our parish or made "suggestions" about my flirting with such and such a guy. She's absolutely blinded by ingrained homophobia.

I guess things could be worse on the Mom-front. I mean, suppose we had money to waste, and I came out to Mom. She would probably want me to do conversion therapy. After all, it's still legal in this state. Yeah, it would be grand to go through that. They probably don't do electric shock therapy anymore. At least I think that's true, just run an electric bolt through you and shock the gayness out. They'd probably just try to pray the gay away and Mom would be in there leading the way on that front. Then when the whole conversion thing didn't work, she'd probably disown me. Maybe she wouldn't. I know she loves me, but who knows what that creepy, awful priest would try to convince her to do.

I do know some gay girls who have come out at school. There's a couple of them I'd really like to date, but they already have girlfriends. Those girls were popular before they came out, though, and their parents are "pillars of the community," so people are going to think twice about messing with them, most people anyway.

I don't know if those girls know I'm gay, though. Would they want to date a gay person of color, one who doesn't have much money? Probably not. Yeah, I've got a lot of things going for me, don't I?

One of the teachers at school has one of those gay/straight alliance-type clubs and they meet once a month on club day. I've heard from Paige, who's a member, that it's really a good club and that the teacher keeps the membership roster a secret. She said that about a sixth of the members are straight like her. How can anything about anything be a secret at a high school? But I really respect the fact that the teacher offered that club and is trying to make people feel safe and wanted. You can bet there weren't clubs like that around ten years ago, so there's been some progress. Maybe I should join that club? I don't know, though. Good old Hannah, you sure can make up your mind about things, can't you?

I'm going to the local college next fall and live at home to save money. I've got a pretty good scholarship "based on need." At least all that studying I've done has paid off, and when I'm there, I'm going to come out for sure. I'm going to take my time about finding a great girlfriend and try to go out with a lot of different people and just see what's out there.

And I'm going to graduate from college with a degree in business and be a successful career woman. I'm a smart and good person, and I've got a lot to offer. And I'm going to let people know that.

31

SCHOOL RESOURCE OFFICER DODD

ONE OF THE BEST THINGS ABOUT MY JOB IS WHEN SOME KID that I had to deal with when he was here comes back to visit after he graduates, and he says that he really appreciated me trying to help him out. There was this one guy that I was so frustrated with about him skipping class that I drove to his house and talked to his mom about why he wasn't in school. The guy was actually hiding under his bed when I found him. Can you believe that?

I took him back to school in my police car and had a long talk with him. That kid ended up graduating. He's serving in the military and doing really well. He always comes to see me when he comes back to visit the school. I really appreciate that.

The worst thing about my job is to see a kid really struggling with drugs or alcohol. They're not dealing with the problem or learning from their mistakes, and it tears me up inside. It's worse when you know that a particular guy or girl is a good person and has ability, but their addiction keeps putting up roadblocks to their success.

I can't force them to change the path they're on, and I know it's not easy to beat an addiction until the kid realizes he has a problem. Some of these kids have the decks stacked against them from the start. They've got no mom or dad in their lives, or the parents or foster parents they do have aren't worth anything, so there's no support system. Then the teachers, guidance counselors, and I have to be the support system. Sometimes we're able to help. Sometimes not—and those times tear me up inside because I felt like I didn't do enough to help.

Then there are those times I get caught in the middle between parents and their kids. There was this senior girl that was 18, and she decided to move out of her parent's house and live with her boyfriend. The guy was no good, and the parents and I knew that, and they wanted me to do something and make the girl come back home, but that girl was legally an adult now and there's nothing the parents or I could do about her living with that guy. Everybody was mad at me—the parents for me not making the girl move back home and the girl for me asking her to consider moving back home. I hope things will work out well with her, but I have this deep fear that she's made a huge mistake that will cost her later on.

Sometimes really good kids get caught up in situations that weren't their fault, and then they make bad decisions, like what happened to Luke and Marcus not too long ago. I got this report from one of my friends on the force that they had been questioned at the mall and accused of shoplifting. Both of those boys would never do anything like that. I know that but the mall people didn't know that. All they saw was a black teen and a white teen dressed in hoodies come into their store, and they assumed the worst.

Marcus comes from a really good family, and everybody knows about Luke's dad and his run-ins with the law, and I know that Luke doesn't want to be judged by his father's problems. That's why I was surprised to hear that both of them boys sort of mouthed off when they were questioned, especially Luke, so I thought I should talk to them about what happened and how they should have handled things.

I told them that it's rough to be in a situation when you know you haven't done anything wrong but then get treated like you have broken the law. I told them probably the only reason they were stopped was because they were young and wearing hoodies. That's not right, but that's the way society—unfortunately—acts.

"It's tough sometimes," I told them, "to keep your anger under control and bite your tongue when you want to say something right back in the worst way, but that's no way to get satisfaction for being unfairly accused of something. You should have reported how unfairly you were treated to the store manager. Then maybe the next time some teen came in dressed all 'wrong,' that guy won't be treated like you were. That's how you get satisfaction."

Marcus next told me that his father had given him "the black father to his black son's talk," and I said that was a very good thing. Then you know, I said, that it's a policeman's job to ask questions, and you just have to answer them in a respectful manner. And you have to hope that they talk to you in a respectful manner.

"I want you to know that I know that some white police officers have done terrible things to black kids," I said. "That's given all of us a bad name, and that's not right either. I can't change the wrongs that other cops have done to many young, black men. There's people in every profession that are just no good."

But for the most part, I said, policemen are just trying to do their job the best way they know how. That's what I'm trying to do at this school.

32

MRS. WHITNEY

MY BIGGEST FRUSTRATION AS A GUIDANCE COUNSELOR IS WHEN I can't get young people the help they need...they deserve. Some of my students have no support at home. I can't change their home lives, but I can try my best to make life better for them here at school. Still, sometimes it's hard to do even that. I've got this one ninth grade boy who lives with his grandparents, the mom has visitation rights but doesn't use them much, and the father is in jail. The grandparents are old and worn out, and they're done with raising kids. They don't even provide a real bed for the boy to sleep on.

Yes, they give the boy food, water, electricity, and a roof to sleep under, but there's no love being given out. I've dropped subtle hints, but I can't make the grandparents care about their grandson. What am I supposed to do?

I feel like I have to deal with some crisis or situation every single day. I have 104 freshmen, exactly 100 sophomores, 93 juniors, and 73 seniors on my caseload. That's 370 kids to keep up with. Before graduation this year, I have to meet with all the seniors and make sure everything is set credit-wise before they leave, and I've got to meet with 76 rising ninth graders from middle school and get them enrolled. How am I supposed to do that if there's a crisis occurring every day? I feel so overwhelmed, and it just never ends. My life is ruled by spreadsheets with kids' names on them. I make lists of things to do, but they never all get done.

The other day I had to tell a senior that he wasn't going to graduate. It was a rough conversation to have to make. I recommended that the boy get his GED instead and go that route. He's a good boy and he has ability, but he just can't pass regular high school tests just like he couldn't pass the state tests. I could see how he was so depressed when I told him the bad news. My fear is that his behavior could spiral down after that, but I felt obligated to tell him what I did. What else could have I done to have kept things from reaching this point? Somebody please tell me the answer to that.

Sometimes when I get home from school, I'm just worn out and don't feel I give my best to my own kids. I've got four between six and 15; they're all two or three years apart. They all have individual needs and are at different stages in life. Some of them have afternoon games or performances, and I want to go to them. But I'm so worn out from school that I just want to go to bed. Sometimes when I do go out to see them at night, I nod off right in the middle of a game or their performance. One of my kids is learning to drive and that's just one more worry.

Next week, all three of us guidance counselors are in classrooms doing suicide risk assessments and talking about crisis situations such as substance abuse. That means a whole lot of my other weekly duties aren't going to get done. I'm being pulled in nine million different directions.

Not everything that happens is bad, though, and those little daily events keep me going...give me hope. The other day Luke came in, and we talked about his plans for college. When I first started working with him, I was so worried that he was going to drop out because that's all he talked about. This year I've helped him with college applications, and it was a great day when he showed me his acceptance letter from the local college. It's so nice to know that I played a part in that. That's an awesome thing. Luke had all these things against him: his mom dying, his dad killed in a car wreck, his grandfather passing away this year, and now he's 18 and living by himself, yet he hung in there and made it through high school. I bet he'll do just fine in college. I told him his life was going to turn out better than he ever realized. I think...I know he believed me. I'm proud that I had a hand in turning his life around.

There are other kids I'm really proud of, too. Marcus was so immature when I started to work with him. He had all these unrealistic expectations about playing professional sports and wouldn't listen to a thing I told him about having a backup plan in case sports didn't work out. Now, he's no longer a football star, but he is one of the brightest young men in the school. I could really see him teaching on the college level or doing research work or maybe working at a museum. Marcus is a success story, too.

Then there are the kids that had every single advantage in life from good homes to wealthy parents and still they messed up, like Caleb. Last year when he was a junior, he started cutting class, blowing up when he was in the classroom, and generally getting into trouble. I really feel he's abusing pills and alcohol at the very least, and there could be more going on in that department, too. He's going to graduate on time, but his GPA has fallen so low and his attitude is so bad that I shudder to think what will happen to him. He's just so agitated all the time.

Still, in spite of everything, I'm glad I became a guidance counselor. I do think I'm making a difference for the better in many kids' lives. I just need to tell myself that at least once every day for my own sanity and peace of mind.

SECOND SEMESTER
BEGINS

33

LUKE

ONE MORE SEMESTER OF HIGH SCHOOL, AND I GRADUATE. That's really hard to believe. I remember one time in ninth grade when Mrs. Burkhead had sent me to Mr. Caldwell's office for like the tenth time, and I told him I couldn't stand going to school anymore. I'd had enough and was going to drop out. But Caldwell said, "High school will be over before you know it. Hang in there." I guess he was right. I'm still here and that hag Burkhead left or quit or whatever after my freshman year.

I'm actually enjoying some of my classes. In U.S. Government, Mr. Martin gave out oral presentation topics the other day for us to work on in our two-person teams. Marcus and I drew one on the most poorly decided cases in Supreme Court history. We're going to research Dred Scott, which held that blacks, whether slaves or free, could never be considered citizens; also Korematsu, which said that it was okay to put Japanese Americans in concentration camps during WWII, and Plessy vs. Ferguson which basically said that Jim Crow laws were fine and dandy. No wonder Marcus wants to be a college professor or historian—this stuff is actually interesting. It's so much better researching stuff on our own than some boring teacher ramming it down our throats in a never-ending, period-long lecture.

In English 12 Honors, we've been reading *Nineteen Eighty-Four*. I had read it before in the book club that Mia and I used to have. The book is all about this world where a Joseph Stalin-type leader runs everything. The book is just as terrifying, just as upsetting, to read for a second time as it was the first time. The most chilling quote is this: "If you want a picture of the future, imagine a boot stamping on a human face—forever." Talk about a dystopia. Page after page has that tone, and it's almost unbearable to keep reading about this horrible world from the future. Who knows, if Hitler hadn't broken his peace deal with Stalin, the world could have ended up like the one in *Nineteen Eighty-Four*.

Statistics and Spanish III have sort of settled into this *D* rhythm. I'm not ever going to understand math, and I'm not ever going to be able to pronounce a whole lot of those Spanish words correctly. And the teachers seem to now understand that. They seem content to just give me a *D* and move on and just shove me up on the stage at graduation. After all, what else could they do with students as dumb as me? It must be depressing for someone who is really good at math or Spanish to be teaching a class with somebody like me in it.

Over Christmas break, Elly came over to my house five or six times at night while her parents were gone to the beach. We also hung out in the day some, hiking up into the mountains or driving somewhere out of the county and having a picnic or something. It was cold doing a lot of those things, but I didn't care and she said she didn't mind.

It's weird, but out of all those things, you know what I enjoyed doing the most with her? Us fixing dinner and sitting down at the table and eating together, and then washing dishes after we were through eating. We've been dating three months now, and it doesn't seem like dating anymore. It just seems like she's supposed to be a part of my life and like she's always been there and always will be.

In high school, the only girls that I've dated that I've ever felt close to were Elly and Mia. They were the only ones I ever really looked forward to being around. Elly makes me feel not lonely and makes this house feel like a home.

I know you could say that maybe I feel that way because I'm lonely since Granddaddy died and that I just like someone for company at the house, but that's not the way it is. I know what real loneliness is like. It's like when I was a tenth grader and Mom had died, and it was just me and Dad at the house, and he was drinking hard and was foul and abusive. School was awful, I was being bullied, and I had nobody to talk to at night except Mia. I'd call her late at night when Dad was at work and tell her what I was going through that particular day. She'd always make me feel better after I talked to her for a little while. That's real loneliness, living in a house with only one other person, like my father, and he wishes you weren't there. You don't want to be around him either, and you're scared of him and thinking of him makes it hard to breathe.

Since Granddaddy died, I don't mind being alone in the house. I'm not lonely and it's because of Elly, because I know I have her to lean on. When Elly comes over, there's like this energy in the house, and it's not a house anymore but a home. I think she feels it, too. At least I hope so. It's just that everything changes when she comes in the door—it's amazing. We've got so much to talk about as soon as she comes in. We might just have seen each other the day before or the afternoon before in Yearbook, but all these things have happened in the meantime, and none of them are really all that important, but we want to talk about them and share what our day's been like. It's just great and it feels so good to talk to her.

It's the same way when we go somewhere. At first, I was afraid that she would mind going to do outdoor stuff with me because she's never been an outdoorsy girl. I finally got up the nerve to ask her if she minded us doing all these outside things. She said she was afraid at first that she wouldn't like going hiking or biking somewhere all the time, but then she realized she was really enjoying herself and it wasn't because she was such a big fan of the outdoors; it was because I was there with her, and she was getting to know me better and better. Then she said, "And I've really enjoyed doing that, Luke. You said that I've been good for you, but you have no idea how good you've been for me."

I swear, it was one of the nicest things a girl has ever said to me...maybe the nicest thing.

34

ELLY

My senior year I've tried so hard to be the person I want to be in my adult life. Not to lie and scheme, but say what I want to say and be honest with people. I'm glad I was the one to ask Luke out for our first date—the old Elly would never have been able to do that. I'm finally in a healthy relationship with a boy who respects me and looks upon me as an equal partner in a relationship.

Luke has been so good for me in other ways. After the first couple times we went tromping around outside, I was exhausted. It was then I realized how physically out of shape I was. A couple of years ago, Mom and I worked out pretty regularly at the club when I was trying to lose weight, but I wasn't going to the club for health purposes. I just wanted to look better in a short skirt. Does the word *airhead* come to mind right about now?

Another great thing about being with Luke is that he has shown me the value of being in good shape, so after a few of those outdoor trips with him, I asked Mom if we could start working out at the gym again, two or three days a week before school. She said sure. Sometimes I walk, sometimes I swim, sometimes I do a little weight-lifting—not heavy stuff but just enough to firm me up a little. Mom only has time to go maybe twice a week, but now I go every morning. Many mornings, I now spend 90 minutes doing things. Some mornings I even walk two to three miles or swim laps for an hour. I've never felt so good about how I look, and I have all this energy throughout the day that I've never had before. I'm not obsessed about my weight anymore, and I honestly think I look better and feel better than ever before. How could I have been so stupid to have binge-purged and done all that extreme dieting stuff when I was younger.

The other day Luke told me how great I looked, and I asked him how he knew. I still want to be complimented, don't all girls? And he then asked me if I had been working out on my own. He could tell! I told him I just wanted to be able to keep up with him when we went to do things. He laughed at that. Then I said I wanted his opinion on one more thing. I said I wanted to tell Mom that he and I had been dating. That I hadn't lied to her about us dating, but I had withheld the truth, that's for sure. I told him that I wasn't ready to tell Dad about us, but maybe I could bring him over for dinner one night when Dad was out of town on business. Luke said to do whatever I thought best, that he trusted my judgment. That's another thing I'm not used to guys saying to me.

So last Tuesday, Dad had to go out of town overnight on a business trip, and I asked Mom if I could have a guy over for dinner. She was really excited about that and asked if it was some boy that she knew. I said yes and then she started listing all those guys from our club or church and, of course, none of them were Luke. I just said she would have to wait until Tuesday night to find out.

About a half hour before Luke was to come, I got sort of panicky about how Mom might act when she saw him, so I decided she had better get over the shock of it being him before he arrived. Mom was shocked when I confessed who was coming and that we had been dating in secret for over three months. "All I'm asking," I told her, "is for you to give him a chance. Ask him questions about anything, what he plans to do in the future, why he wants to be a teacher... just anything."

I'm glad I let her know he was coming because it took a while for that horrified look to leave her face. Then she said, "You're right, I should give him a chance. I don't really know him."

And, boy, did Mom grill him after we sat down for dinner. And she did ask him about his future plans. Of course, Luke said he was going to the local college to study to become a high school teacher, that he wanted to be the kind of teacher who inspired kids to learn and better themselves. He said his grandfather had bought land for him to one day to build a house on and that's where he wanted to live as an adult. I could tell Mom started to soften toward him when he talked that way. When my exes Caleb and Matthew would come over for dinner, they never showed any maturity or common sense. Then Luke started to talk about me.

"I also want to tell you what a wonderful daughter you have," he said. "You already know she's pretty and smart, and, yeah, I like that about her, but the best thing about her is that she has a good heart. That's really rare and special. Elly really helped me get through some tough times when my grandfather died. I just think she's awesome."

After Luke said those things, Mom's whole mood toward him changed. After dessert, it was just small talk until Luke got up to go home. I then walked him to the door and kissed him good-bye. I wanted Mom to see that, too

When Luke left, Mom said she had been all wrong about Luke and apologized for her past attitude against him. "You were right about Luke," she said. "He is different from your other boyfriends. I think you've made a great choice, but I don't think we should tell your father about this relationship...not yet anyway."

Deep down, I fear that it will never be a good time to tell Dad about Luke and me, that Dad will never accept him.

35

MARCUS

I'VE HAD SOME REALLY BIG GAMES IN MY HIGH SCHOOL
football and basketball career, but I've never played so consis-
tently well as I have in basketball this season. It couldn't have
come at a better time for the team, or for me personally, to be
honest. Yeah, I know I'm never going to have the speed and
lateral movement that I had before my leg and head injuries, but
I've got what Joshua calls "ball smarts" now, and I know how to
use them.

Thursday night we had a home game against Northside.
Every year, they're one of the best teams in our district and they
beat us at their place last month. Pregame, Coach Henson told
us we absolutely had to defend our home court against those
guys or we would have no chance at winning the regular season
championship, which would have really hurt us when it came
time to be seeded for the tournament games at the end of the
year. Everybody on the team was psyched up before that talk and
even more so afterwards.

Coach Henson now wants me to rev up the guys after he
finishes the pregame pep talk sort of to emphasize again what
he wants us to concentrate on for offense and defense. I told
everybody that on offense we had to play like a team and work

hard to set screens and picks for guys to get open for jumpers and treys. If they got open, I would feed them. If I had said something about sharing the ball when I was a freshman or sophomore, nobody, and I mean nobody, would have believed me —they would have known it was just BS.

I'm not just leading the team in assists with 8.6 a game though; I'm leading the district in assists. My teammates absolutely know I'll get them the ball if they get open. I'm all about distributing and making sure everybody is getting a touch almost every single possession.

Then I said that on defense they had to fight through screens and make sure they beat their man down court every time. Everybody knew how Northside wants to constantly get out on the break, but that if we shut down their fast break, we could use our size advantage to box them out and make it hard for them to even get off good shots.

The game couldn't have started out any better. I fed Coby for a three right off the tap, and the next time down I made a sweet entrance pass into Garrison for a throw down. Their point sloughed off me on our next possession. He was so afraid that I was going to feed somebody that he gave me all kinds of daylight, so I drained a trey from the top of the key. After that, Northside was so shook up that they didn't know who to concentrate on or whether it was best to try to go zone or play us man-to-man. No point guard is going to be able to contain me when we get off to a start like that.

Heck, I don't think it would have mattered what they did; we went on such a roll. We were up by 24 after the third quarter, and Coach Dell emptied the bench midway through the fourth. On my last possession of the night, I got out on the break, dribbled behind my back to juke the sucker on me, and then blew by him for the slam. Later, I saw Luke and Elly at the game and Elly told me she captured the slam and was for sure going to put it in the basketball spread. Those two are almost always at the home games, Elly taking pictures and Luke interviewing people. But the Yearbook basketball spread is only two pages long and how many interviews and pictures do they need? You know what I think, I think those two are dating on the sly. I've heard other people say that, too.

Anyway, it was good in the fourth quarter for the freshmen and sophomores to get some PT because I'm not going to be here next year, obviously, and I've got to train the guy who's going to replace me. After the game, Coach Henson raved to the team about our play and my senior leadership. Later he came over to me and said I had probably just had the finest all-round game any of his point guards had ever had. Then he said, "If you play like this in preseason practice with the university next fall, they're going to have to give you a scholarship. They won't want to lose you to some team that will give you a free ride." Man, it was good to hear stuff like that.

Friday night, Mom insisted that I go with her and Dad to the winter ball that our club holds every January. She said it was for people of all ages, and I might meet some girl there that doesn't go to my school—that I needed to get out of the house more and do something besides studying and playing hoops. I never would have thought she would have said something like that to me when I was a ninth and tenth grader. Man, I had everything going my way then, ladies- wise.

So I went and ended up spending much of the evening talking with Mia and even danced with her a few times. I was real shocked to see her at the club, but I guess I shouldn't have been. Earlier this winter, Mia had told me her mom was marrying Sai, this really rich guy, in May, and joked that she and her sisters would be "living in luxury." I've been going back and forth on whether to ask Kylee or Mia out or somebody else or nobody; I don't know what I'm going to do. Maybe I should ask Mia out. I think she's still hung up on Luke, but the way Luke and Elly act around each other...

36

MIA

Last Sunday, I finally arranged a time when I could talk alone with Luke. I know I've sounded obsessed about this, but I just had to make sure whether there was anything still between us or whether we could recreate what we once felt for each other. What we came up with is for me to come over for his house for something simple with me bringing dessert.

When I got there around 5:00, he was fixing deer burgers and baked potatoes. I had brought apple pie because I know he likes that. We talked about random stuff while we were eating, but then I decided to just come straight to the point.

"Luke, I know it was a long time ago, but I'm still really sorry about how my father forced me to break up with you at the end of the tenth grade. I know that really hurt you. I know I hurt you when I said I couldn't date you in secret, but I just couldn't go against my father, then. I wish I had disobeyed him, especially the way things worked out, with him running out on us and all."

"It's okay. I understand. I was over it a long time ago," he said.

Did he mean over his disappointment, maybe even over his anger, over us breaking up? Or did he mean over us like in permanently? I waited for him to explain or say something more, but he just paused and sighed. He even turned his eyes away from me. That pause kept growing and growing. Finally, I decided I had waited long enough, waited long enough to come see him, waited long enough for him to explain what he had just meant. I wasn't leaving that house that night without knowing where we stood.

"What do you mean by *over*? Do you mean over us then or over us now?"

He looked up at me and said, "Now, I'm the one not sure what somebody means. What are you asking me?"

I swear, what is it with boys? Luke's got to be the sweetest boy I've ever met, but every boy I've ever met has got a clueless streak in them. Why are they so dense? Again, I tried to come right out and say what I meant.

"What I meant is I still really, really care for you. Before I graduate and go off to college, I've just got to know if you were the one, if you could still be the one. The one guy I was destined to be with, maybe forever. I don't mean to be putting pressure on you, but I've just got to know if there's any hope for us. Whether maybe if we could try dating again to see if those old feelings we had for each other are still there or could be there again. I don't want to be having doubts five, ten years from now that I lost the perfect guy because I didn't speak up when I was a senior in high school."

By then, he was looking straight into my eyes, and I could see hesitation and doubt. I've heard that girls can "read" guys through looking deep into their eyes. It's true; it's really, really true, and I didn't like what I was reading.

"Mia," he said after another too long a pause. "I really care for you still. I'm really, really grateful for what you did for me, giving me self-confidence, helping me with my schoolwork, helping me through those times when Mom was dying and Dad was treating me like dirt. You even brought me things to eat. Not many girls would have done all that. Many, many times during our junior year, I'd think about you, about us, when I was lying in bed at night."

He paused again for a long time, but I could tell he was going to start talking again only when he had chosen his words carefully, so I didn't say anything, I just let him think.

"But," he said and that was the worst word he could have said, and as soon as he said it, I knew there was no chance for us ever again. "But," he started again. "I've moved on. You really hurt me when you said you couldn't date me secretly, and now I realize it was probably for the best. You're going to the best university in the state. I'm going to the small local college.

"After that, you're going to some medical university far away, and I'll still be around here trying to find a teaching job. We'll be far apart and would be apart for a few years. It just wouldn't work out. Besides..."

"Besides what," I said.

"Besides, I'm seeing someone," he said. "I think it's serious. I mean, I really hope it's serious. We haven't said the 'I love you' thing yet, because I've always hated the way adults, kids our age, everybody, throw those words around. I only want to use those words to one girl ever, and I want to make really sure about her and me before I say them, but sometimes it's hard not to say those words to her."

"Oh," I said. "I didn't know. I'm not at school much. I'm sort out of the loop. Is it somebody from school?"

"We've been dating in secret," he said. "She's telling her mom this week. I don't want to talk anymore about it. It's private. I don't know if she'll want people at school to know before we graduate."

"I understand," I said. "Well, I've got to go study."

We talked a little more after that, but I don't remember what we said. I kept my feelings under control until I got home and was in my room, and then I just bawled for who knows how long. Finally, I realized who Luke has to be dating. It has to be Elly. I just know it.

VALENTINE'S DAY WEEK

37

LUKE

There are no secrets in high school, and I guess it was foolish for Elly and me to think that we could hide our relationship all the way to graduation. It was probably more than a little our fault that people figured out we've been dating. I mean, we sit together in Yearbook and English. About every time we pass each other in the hall or somewhere else, we stop to talk. Sometimes, she'll pop into the library during lunch when I'm there and touch base about something we're planning to do together. We've volunteered to "cover" way more boys' and girls' basketball games, girls' volleyball, even swimming matches than anyone would ever expect Yearbook staffers to cover. I know Ms. Hawk must have thought something was going on, but being a teacher she wouldn't have said anything. There must be some sort of rule about teachers commenting on their students' dating lives.

Marcus and Allen have both been pumping me about Elly, sort of like in a "When are you two going to announce that you're a thing. Come on, man" type way. I've tried to play the whole thing off as a joke, but they're not buying it. I can't say I blame them. I can't say I've been very convincing in my...*evasiveness* is the word I guess.

Last Saturday, Elly and I spent all day hiking in the mountains. She brought lunch, and I showed her how easy it is to use water-purifying tablets and straws. It was ice cold all day, and we walked this eight-mile loop trail. When we were planning the trip, I gave her these shorter options for a hike, but she wanted the eight-mile one. She said she'd been really working out hard and wanted a challenge.

I'm really proud of her. She looks great. I mean, it's obvious she's been working out, the way she looks. We were supposed to have gotten back in time for her to go home and shower and change before she went to a sleepover at Paige's house. She'd packed her sleeping bag and other stuff and left it in her car, so as to save time, but we spent too long talking when we broke for lunch, which caused her to have to go straight to Paige's after we got down the mountain. So Elly showed up there with outdoor clothes and hiking boots on, and I guess that was enough to get those girls speculating about where Elly had been all day and who she had been with.

Elly called me Sunday morning and said there was no point in us hiding our relationship anymore. She said as soon as she got to the sleepover late and dressed the way she was, Paige said, "You need to tell Luke to finish up you all's outdoorsy stuff earlier and not make you late for my sleepovers anymore."

Then Hannah chimed in, said Elly, and asked if Luke could take "all of us on a field trip next Saturday." That is, Hannah said, "If you don't mind sharing him." Elly said she laughed at that, and as soon as she did, she knew that was a mistake, because that just confirmed what all those girls were thinking and some of them were saying. So Elly said she "confessed" about us, so we can stop keeping our relationship a secret. She also asked if I was mad at her. I told her of course not. I also told her about the teasing I've been getting from Marcus and Allen.

Later Sunday, I also thought about Mia and felt bad for her. Elly didn't say whether Mia was at that sleepover, but I'm betting she was. That must have been hard for Mia to hear those girls yapping about Elly and me and teasing her on and on. I know I probably hurt Mia when she came over recently. I still feel bad about that and the way things ended with us. I'll always feel bad about it. But I can't change things, you can't change the past.

It didn't take long for the news about Elly and me to be all over school. Elly said it was all over social media, too with Paige and Hannah wanting Elly to post photos of her and me "out in the wilderness" if they weren't "R-rated." I guess it's just a matter of time before her dad finds out. Me and my girl-friends' dads don't tend to get along well, at least from past experience.

Things got a little ugly before Statistics class started on Tues-day, more than a little ugly, really. Two old *buds* of mine, Caleb and Matthew, are in there—two old exes of Elly, too. Before class, Caleb and Matthew came over to me and Caleb said, "I hear you're dating that slut Elly now. You want me and Matthew to tell you about some of our nights with her?"

"Nope," I said and pretended to be super involved with my statistics textbook—which is never the case.

I haven't been able to stand Caleb ever since I met him in middle school—obnoxious little...anyway, who cares about him. I was hoping that those two losers would just leave me alone. Deep down, I knew that would be impossible. Sure enough, they started up again.

"Let me tell you about the night we had together at the beach, oh what a slut she is," said Caleb.

"And let me tell you about our night at a party back in tenth grade," added Matthew. "And how drunk she got and what we did after leaving the party."

I know about those nights, and I don't care about them. I know because Elly told me about them and how screwed up in the head she was back them. How she was attracted to the wrong kind of guy back then—that it was something she guessed she had to go through to know who she really is now.

I started to say something back to them, but then I thought, why give them the pleasure? It's like a little over three months before we graduate. Who cares about high school drama anymore? Meanwhile, there had been a pause in "our conversation," which I guess Caleb couldn't stand.

"Hey, poor white trash, I'm talking to you. Answer me, boy," he said. "You know, maybe I should post something on social media about you and the slut."

With my temper semi under control I said, "Caleb, you must have forgotten that poor white trash like me aren't on social media, so you have my permission to post anything you want about me. If that will make your pathetic little life have more meaning, but... I'd be careful about posting things about Elly. Her daddy's got money and power, and he might not take kindly to you spreading lies about his little girl."

Maybe I did lose my temper right then. Maybe I should have just kept my mouth shut. Then I realized how pathetic a life Caleb lives now. His life has gone downhill since he lost the starting quarterback position his sophomore year. No decent girl will go out with him. The best years of his life have come and gone—wealthy parents, an expensive home, money, a nice car, all the advantages of life—and he blew it; he screwed it all up. Forgive me if I don't feel sorry for him. About that time, Mrs. Roberts finally came back into the room, which was probably a good thing for me because Caleb and Matthew looked like they were about to throw down.

38

ELLY

LAST WEEKEND, LUKE AND I SPENT SATURDAY UP IN THE mountains before I went to a sleepover at Paige's house. I really did a good job of keeping up with Luke all day, and I was still feeling pretty good about that when I got there. So good that I hadn't even thought about how dirty and sweaty I must have looked, especially since I was running a little late which made me the last person to arrive.

I guess that gave everybody plenty of time to gossip and the questions started up as soon as I sat down. "Why are you and Luke always stopping each other in the hall to talk?" "Why are you wearing hiking boots?" "Why do you keep turning us down when we suggest you going out with such and such a guy?" Finally Paige said, "How long have you and Luke been dating on the sly, anyway?"

I was so tired of all the drama and teasing, so I just looked Paige in the eye and said, "About four-and-a-half months." That caused just about everyone to scream, yeah, scream, which sent off another round of teasing and laughing. When all that was going on, I looked over at Mia and she sort of had this forced smile on her face. The rest of the evening was mostly just the same old subjects for conversation: guys, college, senioritis,

when's the next senior skip day, and how many days before graduation. Nobody talks much anymore about what's going on at
school. High school just seems so over, though it's only February.

Like what has almost always been the case at sleepovers over
the years, Mia and I were the last ones to go to bed and we had
one of our after-midnight talks. At first, we had a little, actually a
lot of trouble, getting to the point about what we wanted to talk
about—Luke and me as a couple.

Finally, Mia said, "I am happy for you, Elly. I always figured
that if Luke and I didn't get back together, sooner or later you
and him would, you know, find each other. I was right."

"Thanks for saying that," I said. "I guess I had to find myself
before I found him, or maybe he helped me find myself, but I'm
grateful for you, too, about Luke."

"What do you mean?" she said.

"Because you're the one that helped Luke find himself, that
kept him going his ninth and tenth grade years, which he told
me were the worst years of his life. I was too self-absorbed back
then to have helped him. If you hadn't helped him get through
those years, I bet he would've dropped out. Then there would
have never been a me and Luke. Mia, he told me many times
about how you turned his life around. How much you meant to
him."

"Thank you for saying all that," Mia said. "I am happy for the
two of you. You won't find anybody better."

"I know," I said, but she sure didn't look very happy about
the Luke news, which I can certainly understand; I've got no
problem with that. There was another long pause. Then I said,
"We'd better go to sleep."

The next Saturday was Valentine's Day. On the Monday
before then, Dad *proclaimed* that we were all going to our club's
annual Sweetheart's Dance, probably the club's biggest event of
the year. That night, I wasn't happy about going because Luke
and I had planned to have dinner that night together at his
house. I was going to fix the whole meal.

Obviously I couldn't have taken Luke there. He doesn't have

anything to wear to something like that anyway—and taking Luke and springing that on Dad wouldn't have been a good move anyway. So I was pretty frustrated with the whole we've got to go to the club thing. I called Luke and told him about what had happened, and just like usual, he had a way of fixing things.

"Why don't you fix Valentine's Day lunch for us at my house?" he said. "I've got to clean up the house all morning anyway."

"That's great," I said. Then I added, "Why don't I come over early and help you clean? Your place needs a good cleaning anyway, Luke... really it does. After that's done, we can go grocery shopping, and I'll let you pick out what you want to eat for lunch when we walk through the aisles."

He was all over that idea. Luke's place is neat, don't get me wrong, but it's not clean. I don't think he realizes that. I don't think most guys understand the difference between neat and clean. My two younger brothers certainly don't. You can tell that by the way their rooms look.

Anyway, I got to Luke's house at 8:00 Saturday morning and it took almost three hours to clean the bathroom and vacuum the rooms and get all the stale food out of the fridge—everything was just a mess. It was nice going to the grocery store with him. I mean, don't married couples go to the grocery store on Saturday mornings and run errands together, then? Like almost always when we go do things together, he started teasing me about how I looked at 8:30 in the morning without makeup on. Then I started in on him about how I'd made a big mistake about saying I was going to let him pick out the food for our lunch. I should have just let him go out into some woodlot and let him gather roots and twigs—that he'd have been happy with that type menu.

He let out this huge laugh at that remark and said sassafras roots make very good tea and the next time I came over he would have some all hot and ready for me, but that he doubted "Miss Priss," that's one of his names for me, "would stoop to drinking anything so common."

We ended up laughing and teasing each other the whole time we were at the store and all the way home, too. It was just another great day with him, but things weren't so great when I got home Saturday afternoon. I checked my texts and Paige said that Caleb had posted some horrible stuff, just foul lies, about me, about him and me and why we broke up, on social media.

39

MARCUS

I REALLY DIDN'T WANT TO GO TO OUR CLUB'S ANNUAL Valentine's Day Sweetheart dinner and dance. I mean, it's basically for people my parents' age, though some of the guys and girls from school come every year, especially if they've got nothing else to do—in other words, people like me. I've never felt better about myself and who I am, but my love life has been the pits for months. I just haven't felt like making the effort with high school being so over. Everybody knows that most of the seniors in my class will never see each other again after graduation. It's just the way it is; we'll be scattered all over the country at all kinds of colleges, in the military, going to vocational school, or whatever.

On the way there, my parents said they were sitting with Elly's parents. That's good, because I sure don't want to be around the parents we used to sit with sometimes – Caleb and his folks. Then Dad said that maybe I should try to get to know Elly better, and I laughed at that and said she already has a steady boyfriend. "Oh," said Dad, "I didn't know." Well, I can understand him not knowing, since it's just gotten semi-out about Elly and Luke being a thing.

Anyway, when we got there, I was really surprised to run into Mia. I couldn't believe she was there until I remembered about her mom's engagement to Sai who lives down the street from us. We talked for a little while and then she said that she didn't particularly want to sit with Sai and her mom, who "are constantly flirting and it's so embarrassing." Or sit with her little sisters "who are constantly giggling at everything Mama and Sai say." I said I was down on getting a table of our own.

Mia and me had just started to talk when I saw Caleb walking past where Elly was sitting with my parents and hers, and Caleb gave her the finger. I don't know if Elly's dad saw that or if he just saw Caleb, or maybe he had heard about what Caleb had been posting again about Elly on social media—everybody at school definitely has. Anyway, the man, like, jumped out of his seat and went over to Caleb and just about took off his head with a string of cuss words. The next thing I knew, Caleb's old man flew out of his seat, and he and Elly's dad "were discussing" the finer points of young men who slander young women on social media. For a second, I thought those two guys were going to throw down on each other. I mean, I'd come to these Sweetheart Dances more often if the club would play up the Saturday night is for fighting angle. Finally, after some *well-chosen* words, Elly's dad commented about Caleb's "moral character." Then the two old men went their separate ways. I did hear Elly's dad say "legal action," so I guess things aren't quite over.

Mia and me then shared our opinions on Caleb's character, laughed about that, and ordered. While we were waiting for our meal to come, she asked me if I wanted to dance until the food came and I said sure. The first song was some funky, old person's tune from way back in the 1980s, which made it just about impossible to dance to, but then the band played "As Time Goes By," which Mia and me recognized from when our class did a World War II unit in Ms. Hawks' tenth grade class and watched *Casablanca*. For an old song, it's actually pretty cool. The song is about the desire to love someone who loves you back. How that is universal, and when you really want that one particular person to be yours forever, you've just got to have her or him, "a case of do or die" as the song says.

"As Time Goes By" put both Mia and me in a really deep mood. As she said, "With our high school years just about over, it is a time to be deep and moody. That is, if someone's got enough sense to think about their future."

I agreed and then we started talking about where members of our class would be in ten years, and Mia joked that Caleb would probably be "fat and bald with a big belly and living in his parent's basement and complaining how everybody in the world had been so unfair to him and how it was all *their* fault."

After ragging on Caleb for a while, we both agreed he wasn't worth further discussion. I already know that she wants to be a pediatrician, and she already knows that I want to do something in history, so there was no use in going over that ground again. So I asked her about what she wanted her life to be *like* in ten years, beyond work.

"I want to be married to or about to be married to a man who is intellectually stimulating and strong in character, but at the same time would be gentle and nurturing and encouraging to me and our future kids," she said. "So I guess I'm asking for too much? What do you think?"

"No, you're not asking for too much," I said. "You deserve that. I guess I want the same type of thing from a woman."

We then looked at each other, I mean, like deep into each other's eyes for a long time. And I thought that I must have been crazy not to have at least asked Mia out for a date, but she is so intimidating, she is so smart, she is so beautiful. Why are smart, beautiful girls so intimidating, anyway? But why should that make a difference? Am I afraid to ask a girl out who's clearly smarter than I am, smarter than everybody else in our class? Yet she does seem to really like me.

Finally I said, "Would you like to go out to dinner next Friday night?"

"You mean like on a date, not like this?" she said.

"Yeah, that's exactly what I'm saying," I said. "So what-do-ya say?"

40

MIA

I HADN'T WANTED TO GO TO THE VALENTINE'S DAY DANCE AT Sai's club. I've got too much college and schoolwork to waste spending a night out with Sai, Mama, and my sisters. But at the last moment, Mama convinced me to go, so I did. I figured I could use a night out and be away from my studying for a while.

I ended up sitting with Marcus, basically out of pure random chance. We started talking about deep stuff like what would we be doing in ten years, and the next thing I knew, he asked me out for a dinner date. I mean the guy who Camila, Hannah, and I, especially, used to make fun of the whole time we were ninth graders because he was so immature. That guy asked me out, and I said yes and I was actually thrilled that he thought I was somebody that he would want to go out with a time or two, or maybe more. I don't know, yet.

People do change over the course of their high school years. I know Marcus has. He has grown up. He has gotten a lot more mature. He cares about things worth caring about: racial relations, injustice, countries stupidly repeating stupid stuff from their history, politicians fear mongering, and trying to play to people's worse instincts and fears. Marcus has always been good looking, so there's that. But he was good looking as a ninth grader, too, and I would have laughed at even the suggestion I might have ever gone out with him.

"So where do you want to go out to eat?" I asked. "It'd better be somewhere super nice because I am so used to the finer restaurants in this area."

Which, of course, I'm not used to at all, which probably explains why he laughed so loud. I'm not used to swanky places. I never expected to be eating at the club, either, and there I was, too.

"How about us driving up to the university Saturday afternoon," he said. "We can walk around the campus and town for a while, go out dinner somewhere nice, and then we can go to the basketball game that night. I can probably get a pass for the two of us. How does that sound?

"Not bad," I said. "Not bad at all, I guess you've convinced me."

I was trying to play things cool, but I was really excited about going up there with him. Mama was too when I told her. She said she would take me shopping for a nice dress Monday after school, and I told her that we couldn't afford that. Then she said that Sai had given her a charge card and that she could use it from time to time if she needed to, and this was one of those "needed to" times.

The whole getting ready for the date thing was weird. I wasn't used to just going out and buying something nice like that dress—I mean just going out and buying something as a luxury without even worrying about it. No wonder so many kids who grow up being able to do things like that don't appreciate things. Don't understand how people like me and my family struggle just to have basic stuff and can't comprehend buying things almost on a whim.

Marcus and I certainly didn't have trouble talking about things on the way up to the university. In fact, we had lots of things to talk about the whole time. He was all wound up about a history paper he's working on about Geronimo. How he was one of the last Native Americans to come under the control of the military. "Like the man fought invaders for decades and terrorized American and Mexican authorities the whole time," he said. "Then Geronimo died of old age in his 90s in the early twentieth century. Can you imagine that? The odds of him surviving all those battles and then dying of old age, amazing."

I told him I hadn't known that he had attacked Mexicans, and then we started speculating whether my ancestors were involved in those raids. Who knows? Later, we walked around the campus for a while. It was good to get more familiar with things. Every time I've been up there, I've gotten more comfortable with where things are. I'm going to be so busy with my school work and stressing about that. I don't need to be stressing about how long it takes to walk from my dorm room to the cafeteria or in what buildings my classes are.

Then it was time for dinner and we ended up this restaurant that serves all these expensive seafood and beef dishes and Marcus suggested why didn't we have the two-person lobster entrée. I've never had lobster before, so I thought why not. At dinner, he wanted to know all about the classes I was going to have to take next year and how those classes would fit in with my pediatrician career. I talked and talked about that, and he was listening and asking questions the whole time. I kept thinking about how much Marcus has changed.

At the game, we sat right behind the player's bench. Before the game started, some of the players were nodding toward Marcus and saying things like, "Go suit up, we could use you tonight," and "I'll text you when we have some pickup games this summer. Maybe you can come up and play." I could tell Marcus was really pleased about how they were acknowledging him.

When the game started, I actually got caught up in things. I mean, after all, this is soon going to be my school. I ended up cheering like everyone else did. We won in a rout. On the way home, Marcus talked nonstop about what had gone on and was explaining why such and such a play was called. I had a really, really good time. I didn't mind one bit when he kissed me goodnight.

MARCH MADNESS

41

LUKE

"Dad's found out about us," was what Elly blurted out when she sat down next to me in first period, Friday. "He told me to ask you to come over to our house tonight to talk with him and Mom. I would have called you last night to tell you, but I was worried that it would upset you. I just had to tell you in person."

I didn't say anything back to her at first. I knew this day was coming, the come on over to the house and talk to the parents thing, and I've been dreading it, the whole five-and-a-half months we've been dating. Next, the thing I feared most came into my head. I bet Elly's dad has already told her, ordered her, to break up with me.

"Did he tell you to break up with me?" I asked.

Then it was time for Elly to have a long pause. "Yes," she finally said. "But, Luke, you don't have to worry about me ever breaking up with you. I want you to really, really know that. I... you know how I feel about you...about us."

She stopped and looked at me for like what seemed like a long time, and then she teared up. I reached over to her and rubbed her back. I looked up and saw Ms. Roche looking at us and she said, "Do you all need to go out in the hall?"

"No," I said.

"Yes, please," Elly said, so out we went.

"Everything's going to be okay," Elly said. "Mom's on our side. She wasn't at first, you know that, but now she is. Besides, it doesn't matter what he wants or what he's going to say Friday night. I'm in...I'm..." Then she started crying, really hard.

I just wanted her to stop crying, so I tried to think of something to say, anything, "Does he want me to come for dinner?"

"No, not for dinner," she said. "Come over after dinner, around 7:00."

Of course the old man doesn't want me coming for dinner. He doesn't want somebody like me at his table. I'm not good enough to eat at his table, date his daughter, converse with his wife, and talk to him man to man. I was good enough to mow his lawn back in the day, that's about it, but putting my lower class hands on his wife's dishes, my lower class lips on his nice, fine glasses, well that's just too much for him to take.

Bitterness, anger, rage were just washing all over me, but then I decided not to let that happen. I'm not going to let that man get to me, bring me down. Yeah, it's going to be bad Friday night, but I'm going to go into that man's house and act like a proud, confident man myself, because I am somebody...screw him.

"What are you thinking, Luke?" Elly said. "Are you okay?"

Right then, I wanted to tell her that I love her. I've been thinking about saying it because that's the way I feel about her, but out in the hall in first period is not where I'm going to say it for the first time. It has to be a special moment, not a moment when I'm all mad inside at her dad and when we've got to go inside the classroom because first period English has started.

My dad never told me he loved me, not once. Mom every now and then said she loved me. I know that she did, but she was just not good at saying it. Granddaddy never said he loved me, and I never said it to him, either, but I know that we loved each other. I guess some families just don't seem to be able to express themselves that way.

Or is this just something that guys are bad at, saying that we love somebody? Or was my family just screwed up in the head that way? Were Mom and Dad and me just so poor and worried all the time about having enough money to get by that we forgot about important things? Like saying we loved each other? I don't know.

But all that's in the past. There is no mom, dad, and grand-daddy anymore...no family anymore. It's just me... and Elly...I hope forever.

"Luke, answer me," Elly said again, snapping me back to reality. "Are you okay?"

"That's just like you," I said. "You're crying and then you stop because you're worried about me. That's why you mean so much to me. That's just one of many reasons why you mean so much to me."

"Thank you," she said. "You mean so much to me, you have no idea how much you mean to me." She then paused for a while. "I just want to say that I...I guess we'd better get back to class. The A.P. exam will be here before we know it, and that's a college credit for both of us if we pass it. I think Ms. Roche said she was going to go over some pretty important stuff, today."

"You're right," I said, "Let's go in."

"First, you have to kiss me," she smiled.

"Nope, can't do it, against school policy...public displays of affection. No PDAs, that's what the student handbook says, and we must live our lives by the student handbook. I'm not going to get suspended because of some girl. No sir. The next thing you know, you're going to be wanting to wear a hat on your head around school and wearing dresses eight inches above your knees and those shirts where there are little slits showing your upper arms. It's a slippery slope, Elly, a slippery slope that we're not going to go down."

"Is that what they call senior sarcasm?" she laughed.

"A senior being sarcastic his senior year, Elly, Elly, shame on you," I said.

I had made her laugh, that was good. But I wasn't looking forward to Friday night, that's for sure.

42

ELLY

"Elly, do you want to explain to me why I had to find out through social media that you've been dating some boy behind my back," was the first thing Dad said to me when he got home Thursday night. He then followed up that little bit of sarcasm with this little jewel: "What on earth, little girl, do you see in a boy like Luke? You know what he is, where he came from."

He hurt me when he said that, but he also made me mad. I said, "Yes, Daddy, I know what he is: kind, decent, loving, honest... let me think, what else? How about hard working and mature, too? Basically, all the things Caleb wasn't. Surely you remember Caleb, the boy you liked so much that was kicked off the football team... that physically and emotionally assaulted me... that's been suspended a whole bunch of times...that spends his nights—and mornings—and part of his time in school, drinking and popping pills. Remember him, the ideal man for me you kept saying, or how about all those other boys that were from the right neighborhoods and right families: Matthew, Jonathan, Paul. You know, the boys you liked so much that weren't right for me."

"Enough!" Dad shouted. "Don't take that tone with me."

"Both of you stop," Mom interrupted, and I was really glad she did. "Luke's been over here since they've been dating, and I approve of their relationship." Then she looked at Dad and said, "I think you need to give this boy a chance. I'll tell you one thing. He has more depth, more maturity, than most boys his age. Elly told me what Luke has gone through."

"So how long have you known about them dating and why didn't you tell me," said Dad to Mom. "Can you explain that?"

"We've been dating since early October and Mom has known for several months," I interrupted. "Mom and me just thought you weren't ready to hear about it."

"You've got that last part right, little girl," he said. "Has he told you he loves you, have you two...?" then his voice trailed off and I knew what he was hinting at.

"No, he hasn't told me he loves me and no we haven't," I said.

"I want you to break up with him," Dad said.

"No way," I said. Then I paused and said, "I haven't told him yet that I love him, but I'm going to tell you and Mom right now that I do, and I know that he loves me, too. He just hasn't said it, yet."

"Elly, I swear, girl, you are throwing your life away," Dad said. "You have no idea how big, how huge, a mistake you're making. You'd better listen to me. You'd better stop..."

"No, you're the one that had better stop," Mom interrupted. Then she turned to me. "Elly, I want you to invite Luke over for dinner tomorrow night so we can all talk, and your father can get to know the real Luke."

"That boy," and Dad just spit out the word *boy*, "is not going to eat at my table."

"That boy has already eaten at *our* table," Mom snapped right back. "But fine if you don't want to eat with him. Elly, tell Luke to come over after dinner around 7."

"I will," I said.

I felt all tense that night at dinner. I hardly slept all night.

The next morning it was just awful telling Luke about some of what had happened Thursday night. When Friday night rolled around and Luke came over, Dad just glowered at him when he came into the living room. My little brothers had wanted to stay in the living room because in their stupid male heads they knew something was up. But Mom sent them to their rooms with a tone that said don't argue with me.

I was expecting Dad to light into Luke right away, but he just seemed too mad to even talk. Nobody said anything for the longest time, and then Mom finally said something lame to Luke like, "Well, not long to graduation is it? What are you going to be doing this summer?"

"I haven't even told Elly this, yet, but I just found out today that I could swing going to summer school at the local college," he said. "I'm going to take two classes. If I take two classes each summer for the next three years and maybe take an independent study or two, I can graduate in three years. Then hopefully get a teaching job around here somewhere. My grandfather bought some land for me before he died. I'm planning to build a house there after college. Hopefully everything will work out for all that to happen."

When Luke said all that, I almost jumped right up and kissed him, but all I did was smile and look Dad in the eye. Come on, Daddy dearest, say something to all that. Explain to me how a boy who has done all this deep thinking and planning would say something like that and just has to be a no-good loser.

"Why, Luke," Mom said. "That sounds wonderful. I'm really impressed you've thought so far ahead in life."

"Building a house takes a lot of money," Dad said.

"I've been saving for years," Luke said. "Plus, I would sell Granddaddy's house. The land's already paid off, so the way I figure it, the money from his house and what I've saved would be enough to get the house started, and I'll be working part time all the way through college. So I hope, I think, things would work out. What do you think, sir?"

Luke looked at Dad when he said that. All Dad did was mumble something that I couldn't hear. I don't remember much about what we talked about after that. All I could think about was how I hoped Luke would want to take me to his land soon, and what it would be like to maybe live with him there one day.

43

MARCUS

I LOVE MARCH COLLEGE BASKETBALL AND THE NCAA tournament—the win and move on or lose and go home mindset —but I've never gotten to experience real March Madness on my level, until now. At school, we've had some good teams in the four years I've played, but this year, it's like, you know the saying: we "caught lightning in a barrel." We started out slow in November and December, but in January and February, we just hit our stride. When Coach Dell moved me to point guard before the season started, it was the best thing that has ever happened to my high school sports career. I felt like I just took control of the team and helped those underclassmen like Garrison and Coby hit their strides.

We won our conference tournament and then upset a bunch of teams in the regionals; then all of a sudden, it's mid-March and we're in the final four at the state tournament. I mean it was just surreal. Nobody expected us to go that far. I think even Coach Henson was more than a little surprised. He just kept saying, "Ride the wave, gentleman. We'll see where it takes us." The guys were a little more vocal. Our big saying was "Shock the world, one more time." I liked that us against the world mentality. It really helped us bond.

Thursday at school, we had a pep rally before we got on the bus to the state capital for that night's game. Coach Henson had arranged it so that the athletic director, Mr. Pound, called us up one by one in front of the student body. That way, each one of us got to be individually cheered for. Man, that was something. The senior section was just rocking when their fellow seniors were called up. Then it was time for us to get on the bus, get to the capital, have a pregame meal, and do a shoot around. The school arranged for several buses to take students down to the game, and a lot of the upperclassmen drove down. Mia went down with Hannah, Paige, and Leigh. Luke told me that Ms. Hawk told him and Elly to go to the game and devote a whole Yearbook spread to just the state championship tournament and all the stuff that went along with it.

Thursday night, we played Lawrenceville, some team from down on the coast. They were some big-looking dudes and all their starters were seniors or juniors. Two of the seniors had already gotten D-I scholarships and the third starting senior had gotten a scholarship to a D-II school, so I knew we were up against it from the start. I mean, I'm the only senior starter on our team and all I've got is a walk-on commitment. I think the guys were more than a little intimidated that Lawrenceville's starting five was so much older than us. They were a lot bigger, too. The only place we had a size advantage was at point guard. Their junior starter was a good three inches shorter than me.

Basketball is such a head game, and I could tell that Coach Henson realized some of the younger guys were a little... I don't want to use the word *scared*, but, face it, they had that look on their faces before the game started. But right before we left the locker room to start the game, Coach said just the right thing to settle us down.

"Everybody out in the stands thinks we're going to lose. All the college scouts here think that's what's going to happen, but the best thing that we have going for us is that Lawrenceville's players think they've already won this game. They've read all the stuff in the paper and online about how great they are. They're just playing this game to get it out of the way before they play in their real game for the state championship game Saturday night."

Henson just spit out the phrase *real game*. Then he ended up his talk with his final instructions. "But we're going to come out and kick 'em in the gut right off the tap. They're going to be 10 points down before they know it, because I believe in you guys. Then they're going to tense up because their losing shouldn't be happening, and they'll start firing up wild shots, and it'll just get worse for them. That's how we're going to win this game!"

What a talk! Right before we ran out onto the court, Coach Henson took me aside and talked to me. "You're going to go off for a triple double, Marcus. Their point guard is too short to play you and you're going to start out driving by him and setting up the guys for easy baskets. Then he's going to play off of you, and then you're going to burn him with threes. Got that?" Then after a pause, he said, "Later on, when he's so screwed up in the head from what you've been doing to him, you're going to post up and shoot over him, and if you get doubled, you'll dish to one of the guys."

It was like Coach Henson had the whole game planned out, and he was so confident in me that it made me feel like I was unstoppable, and the game went pretty much just like Henson said it would be. Lawrenceville's guys were all cocky when we shook hands before the tap, sort of having this smirk on their faces. I got the ball off the tap, and I hit a streaking Garrison in stride for a slam. I picked their point on their first possession, and then it was my turn to slam one home.

They turned the rock over again on the very next possession, and on the fast break, I saw Coby over on the right baseline. I dished it to him, and my man hit a three. Their coach started yelling at them, but he wouldn't call a timeout which was a big mistake. I pressured their junior point on the next possession, picking him up before he even reached mid-court. He panicked and threw the ball away, and I hit a long three like seconds later.

The guy was so out of it from his turnover that he left me free at the top of the key.

We were up 10 at that point, and that's how many points we won by. We're playing in the state championship game Saturday night. Can you believe that! Oh, by the way, just like Coach Henson said, I got my triple double: 20-10-12.

44

MIA

ME GOING TO A HIGH SCHOOL BASKETBALL GAME, CAN YOU imagine that? Old Mia who has been in high school for four years and who has spent all her time grinding away and never really doing much of anything that wasn't school, studies, and grade related goes off to a game to see her boyfriend play in a state championship tournament.

Yeah, I guess I can call Marcus, Marcus of all people, my boyfriend. We've been dating for a month now, and it's been really good. We've only been out on four dates. He's been so busy with basketball and I've been so overwhelmed with finishing up my college and high school classes that those four dates have been all the time we've had to be together.

Marcus has really changed since he was a ninth grader. He has *depth* to him, an intellectual curiosity that I never thought he would have when I first met him. It has been nice having a guy to talk to, to vent about things in school that weren't going well, to talk to about current events. I mean, this guy is really well-read. He's always reading some book about history, and he wants to tell me about what he's read. You know what, I want to hear about things like that because they are interesting. I can't stand to be around stupid boys, and Marcus is really smart. That's another thing that I thought I would never say about him.

Paige, Hannah, Leigh, and I went to the game Thursday together, and then after the team won on Thursday, we drove back on Saturday night for the championship game. I should say that I drove. That's another thing that's hard to believe. With Sai and Mama getting married in just six weeks, they've already started pooling their resources. Well, I should say, he's started to give Mama money for things. My family doesn't have much resources to pool. One of the things that Sai has given Mama is a new car. When my friends found out about that, they all begged for me to drive them down for the game because I had a better car than everybody else did. So on Thursday and Saturday nights, I drove three girls for three hours down the interstate and three hours back up to see a boy, my boyfriend, play a game based on the premise that you throw a ball into a basket. And if you do that a whole bunch of times, you win. Just surreal. I still don't understand why they call basketball this time of year March Madness. Maybe it's because the teams are mad at each other or the referees?

Friday night, in between the game nights, Marcus and I went out to dinner for our fifth date. I figured he would want to talk about basketball all night, but instead he wanted to know all about what I'd been studying at college. Then when we had exhausted that topic, he had to tell me all about a book he was reading on the Japanese internment in World War II. The whole night I felt I was talking to somebody who is just as smart as I am.

I saw Luke and Elly at the games both nights. I'm finally over the jealousy thing toward Elly. I'm ashamed to admit that I was jealous, but I was for a long time. Even Ms. Perfect, High School Valedictorian is allowed to have one little human flaw. The way they look together, the way she touches him, the way they talk, it's obvious that they're into each other in a big way. Well, good for Elly, good for Luke, good for them both.

The championship game Saturday night was not so good; it

was a blowout. At least that's the word Marcus used to describe the game. He texted me late Saturday night after everybody had gotten back home, so I called him back. I guess he figured I would be up late catching up on my studying, which I was.

I thought Marcus would be really down after losing the state championship game by like 20 points, but, no, he said Coach Henson in the locker room after the game really praised the team and told them how proud he was of them. How they had been the first basketball team in school history to play for a state championship. That dozens of teams around the state had had their seasons over weeks and weeks ago, and that the team had, indeed, "shocked the world" as Henson put it.

I told Marcus that it appeared to me that he had played very well, but he said he didn't want to talk about how he played because the team had lost. That he was the quarterback of the team, and the burden of losing fell on him. He then started beating himself up and talked about the turnovers he had and how that had changed the game.

After we got off the phone, I looked up the game online and found that Marcus had had what the sportswriter called "a triple double," which is, from the way the writer wrote, really impressive. I read on and learned that Marcus was the first person in state high school history to have triple doubles in both final four games, so I think Marcus was being too hard on himself.

The next morning I texted him and wrote, "Congratulations on the triple double. You should have told me about that last night." He texted me right back, "How about a drive out in the country and a picnic lunch. Down for that?" I called him and said he was assuming a whole lot about me not having a date on a Sunday morning, and he laughed about that and said, "Do you want to go on a picnic or not?" I said I did, and we did have a really good time. I need to enjoy my last days of high school a little. My academic career won't come to an end if I relax a little bit.

SENIOR SKIP DAY IN APRIL

45

LUKE

"WHAT ARE WE GOING TO DO ON SENIOR SKIP DAY?" WAS what Elly asked when she sat down next to me in first period English on Wednesday. I didn't know there was a senior skip day on Friday. I guess if there's been one constant in my four years of high school, it's been that I've been clueless about just about everything that's going on or about to happen.

"You didn't know about it, did you?" she said. "I can tell by the look on your face." Then she started teasing me about how she couldn't believe she was dating a boy who was "so out of it all the time." After a little while of pretending to humiliate me she turned serious and said, "Actually, that's one of the reasons I am dating you. You care about all the important things, the things that matter." She squeezed my hand when she said that, and I made three decisions right then.

I went up to Ms. Roche and asked her what was planned for Friday in class, and she said nothing, it was senior skip day, so even a teacher knew more about what's going on than I do. I asked her if she could give me some extra help that day on planning for the English A.P. exam. I want that freshman English credit before I go to college. I want it bad. That's one of the things I want to accomplish so I can graduate from college in three years and get on with my life. I told Ms. Roche all that, and she said she would be glad to give me some writing prompts and sample short answer questions that day.

When I got back to my desk, Elly said, "So we're going to be sitting in first period English on senior skip day? Boy, you'd better make the rest of the day special."

"Actually, I was planning to, girl." I said right back and that's when I told her about the second thing I'd decided. "I've been needing to cut wood for the winter to save on my electric bill. How about going up to the land with me to help do that. You haven't seen it yet. We'll take my pickup instead of your baby blue Prius which probably wasn't made for hauling wood."

"Luke, I'd absolutely love to go see your land," she said. "I've been really curious about it. It's what, a 30-minute drive from town? How about if I make a picnic lunch? How long do you think it will take to cut the wood? What do you want to do afterwards?"

"You're right, it's 30 minutes or so," I said. "Yeah, make lunch. I think it'll take a couple hours to fill up the truck. Since you're helping me in the morning, I'll let you decide what we'll do in the afternoon."

That's one of the many things I like about her. She does want to help me with things. She's changed a lot, I've changed a lot. We've helped each other grow up. I know she believes all that, because she's told me I've helped her to change. She's said over and over how she never stresses out over her weight and looks and makeup and all those unimportant things like she used to her first three years of high school.

I think she's always looked great; she just didn't believe in herself. I also know that Mia and Elly helped me become a man. I know what I want out of life now because of them. The third decision I made Wednesday morning is that Friday when we get up to the land, the first thing I'm going to do is show her the whole 30 acres.

We're going to walk to the creek that forms the back end of the property where it meets the national forest. Then I'm going to show her that beautiful mature forest hollow with all those big white oaks. Next, I'm going to take her to that little flat place near the hollow where I want to build a house after college. And after that, I'm going to tell her that I love her.

I've been wanting to say it for about a month now. I've had strong feelings for her even before we had our first date last October. They're just gotten stronger and stronger. You know what? I think, no, I'm sure she loves me, too. I think she's been waiting for me to say it, or hoping I would, or something like that.

I know telling a girl you love her before you ask her to help you cut firewood isn't the most romantic thing in the world, but I don't care about all that.

After Wednesday, Friday couldn't come soon enough. Ms. Roche had a lot of stuff for Elly and me to do in our two-person class that day. Yep, of course, nobody else showed up. I felt like I aced the writing prompt that Ms. Roche gave us. I felt real good about the short answer questions, too. Right after class, Elly and I headed for the mountains.

It's funny. We usually talk nonstop when we go anywhere, but on the drive there, neither one of us hardly said anything. It wasn't tense or anything between us. She seemed to be deep in thought like I was. When we got there, I did everything pretty much like I'd planned. I showed her the creek, the property boundary, the hollow, and then the flat where a house could be.

She got really enthusiastic about the home site, saying how perfect it was and how you would be able to see the morning sun come up out the front window if the house was built a certain way. That's when I said, "I just wanted to tell you that I love you."

46

ELLY

I REALLY WANTED TO SEE LUKE'S LAND. I WAS THRILLED WHEN
he said on Wednesday that was where he wanted to take me on
senior skip day. I teased him a little that going out in the forest
wasn't my idea of a romantic day trip with a guy, but then I
stopped talking that way because I was afraid he'd change his
mind and take me somewhere else.

I've been fantasizing about living there with Luke. I've been
doing that so much that I can't keep it out of mind. But the
most important thing is I've wanted to tell Luke that I love him.
I do really think this is true love. We've been dating for over six
months now and have settled into this really sweet, comfortable
relationship. Most Friday nights I go over to his house and cook
dinner. Saturdays we usually go do something outdoors. Sundays
after lunch he comes over to my house, and we go walking for a
couple of hours, and it never gets old being around him—always
something to talk about, always something to discuss.

On the way up to his land Friday, neither one of us talked
much, which was really unusual with us. I kept debating over
and over whether I should tell him I loved him while we were
in the car or wait until we got there. I had decided I was definitely going to say it that day. I had been wanting him to say it

first. I know that sounds like a stupid girl thing, and it was stupid of me to be like that. That's why I was going to tell him I loved him, even it meant me saying it first. After all, I asked him out for our first date, and that turned out pretty good, didn't it?

When we got there, Luke was like this whirlwind. He had to show me just everything about the land. He took me to the creek and the edge of the national forest. He showed me all these beautiful mature oaks. The last place we went was the home site and that's where he told me he loved me for the first time.

"Oh, Luke," I said and started crying. I couldn't help it. I was so happy. Then I started just sobbing so hard that I couldn't stop.

Then he said, "I'm sorry, Elly, I didn't mean to upset you," and he had this hurt look on his face.

"No, Luke, you didn't upset me," I said. "I'm crying because I'm so happy. Don't try to understand it. It's just me. I'm also crying because I wanted to tell you today that I love you. You just beat me to it."

He smiled at me, took my hand, and walked me over to this huge tree and kissed me.

"Let's sit down against the tree and talk," he said, and we did, for way over an hour. I put my head on his shoulder, and he wrapped his arm around me, and we just talked. He said what kind of house would I like to live in one day because he didn't know much about that type of thing because he had only lived in his parents' and grandfather's houses. They were so small and everything was so crowded that he didn't know what a house needed to be like.

I told him I wanted a brick house with two stories, one that had lots of space and a garage for both cars. Plus, I wanted a big backyard, so our kids would have plenty of room to play. Then I thought I shouldn't have said something so bold like that, but he said, "Yeah, our kids would need a big yard. That makes sense."

He paused for a little while and then started joking with me.

"You think because I used to mow your dad's lawn that I wouldn't mind mowing a big yard, don't you?"

"Well, you are a trained lawn boy," I teased right back. "There's got to be some kind of reason why I would consider marrying you. It's not because you're a suave, sophisticated man about town, that's for sure. Just don't mow down the flowers in my flower garden. Lawn boys are sometimes careless about things like that."

"Well, Miss Priss," he said. "I can't imagine you getting your hands dirty enough to plant a flower garden."

"You're right about that, Mr. Lawn Boy," I said. "You're going to plant my flower garden for me. You're also going to weed it for me every week. But I'm the only one who gets to pick the flowers for the vase on the kitchen table."

"Oh, so now you've got all that planned out, too," Luke said.

"I most certainly do, Mr. Lawn Boy," I said. "I'm going to keep you so busy with chores that you won't have time to do anything else."

We both started laughing again, and things then turned serious. Luke started talking about the classes we would take in college and how we both could graduate in three years and get our teaching certificates.

Finally he said, "I don't think we should tell anybody about all this yet, especially your parents."

"I agree," I said. "I think we should wait, maybe...how about partway through our second year of college?"

"That makes sense," he said. "That would give me plenty of time to put some extra money away for your engagement ring."

"Oh, Luke, I don't need any engagement ring," I said.

"I need for you to have one, though," he said. "It's important to me."

I admit that I was glad he wanted to buy me an engagement ring, but since he knows so little about things like that, I could for sure steer him toward buying one that wouldn't be very expensive.

"Well, let's get started with the wood cutting," he said. "I might as well cut a couple of trees down where the house is going to be."

I felt like I was walking on air the rest of the day, even when I was carrying wood to his pickup. It was the best day of my life. My whole relationship with him has been a series of best days of my life-type days.

47

MARCUS

"Marcus, I can't swim," was what Mia said to me when I asked her if she wanted to go to the lake with me on senior skip day. Allen had said he and Paige (I'm glad they've patched things up) were going to the lake and wanted to know if Mia and me would like to come, too. Allen said we could rent some paddle boats at the marina and float around in one of the coves nearby. Then maybe eat lunch at the marina and maybe go play some miniature golf in the afternoon. Come dinnertime, go get some pizza or something—make a day of it.

It all sounded great until Mia said she couldn't swim.

"We'd be in a boat," I said. "I wouldn't turn it over."

"But what if I fell out," she said. "It's April; the water is still cold. I could get hypothermia. I've never had any swimming lessons. I've never owned anything to go swimming in."

Once again, I realized how different Mia's life has been compared to mine. I mean, I knew about the poverty she's grown up in; how her father ran out on them; how her family lived a lot of different places, but nowhere as long as the place they're living at now. How it's going to be weird when her mom gets married next month to a rich guy, and she and her sisters for the first time aren't all going to be sharing the same bathroom every morning. How they are going to have their own bathroom inside their own bedroom.

I had swimming lessons at the club when I was really little. When I was rehabbing my knee, I would swim. It's just something that most people know how to do.

All that was going through my head when she added, "Marcus, I do want to spend the day with you, that would be great, but there is no senior skip day at college. I've got to go to my morning classes. Why don't you come over to my house at 1:00 after I've gotten home and eaten lunch? Then we can go do something."

"How about me taking you to the club and giving you swimming lessons?" I said.

"Marcus, wow, I'd really appreciate that," she said. "That would be so sweet of you. I could ask mom for some money to buy a swimsuit."

In my head, I got this image of Mia wearing a bikini, which was a pretty good thought to have. "Great," I said, "I'll pick you up at 1:00."

It was great until I started thinking about how could I teach the valedictorian of the class, the smartest student in the whole school, how to do something. I went online and all the how-to suggestions were for teaching a kid to swim—things like "make it fun, sing songs," junk like that. Finally, I found something that said to start people out by showing them how to blow bubbles, then how to turn their heads from side to side, next how to kick. The next step was to put someone on a kickboard and show her how easy it is to kick and float around. I decided all that would be enough for the first lesson.

Things couldn't have gone better at the pool, and, yes, Mia did show up in a bikini. She immediately caught on to everything I told her to do. Before we left, she was able to float a little. I don't think there's anything this girl couldn't quickly learn how to do. She even asked if I could give her some more lessons next Friday after school. I said fair enough if she would agree to go out with me to dinner afterwards.

"I guess so," she said and smiled. "It will be a sacrifice of my time, but I guess I can give up some studying time. Where are we going next?"

I had never even thought about that so I asked her what other kind of sports had she never done.

"I've never gone bowling," she said. "In ninth grade, when all the other Phys Ed students went on the bowling field trip, I stayed at school and worked. I didn't have the money to go on the trip. Besides, I figured I could stay at school and get ahead on my homework for that night."

So I took her to the local bowling alley and showed her how to bowl. I'm not very good at bowling, but at least I know how to. I usually score about 150 or so when I go. The best part about our bowling alley trip was me holding her arm and showing her how to walk and sort of glide down the lane and release the ball.

She caught on to the whole bowling thing just as quickly as she did the swimming. She made a 120 and said the most amazing thing. "There's a lot of physics in this," Mia said. "Plus there's some geometry, too, in the way you have to play the angles between the ball's point of release and impact on the pins."

I bet if we ever go bowling again, she'll outscore me. Her superior intelligence comes through in everything she does. If I had gone out with her before our senior year, her intelligence would have intimidated me. Maybe that's why some guys don't like to date really smart girls? They can't bear the thought of someone being a lot smarter than they are. After we went bowling, I asked her if she wanted to go out to dinner. She said no, that I had spent enough money on her for the evening. "How about," she said," going to your house and just hanging out? Mama is having her fiancé over for dinner tonight at my house, so we can't go there."

I was down with that because Mom had been saying she wanted to get to know Mia better. So I called Mom and asked if I could bring Mia to the house for dinner, nothing too fancy because it was so short notice. Mom practically shrieked "Yes" over the phone. Of course, Mia really charmed Mom which isn't surprising. It was one of the best days I've ever had, and I hardly spent any money. I wish I could have learned earlier the lesson that the quality of the person you're with is more important than the quantity of money you spend.

48

MIA

WHEN MARCUS ASKED ME TO GO TO THE LAKE WITH HIM ON senior skip day, I was really glad that he wanted to spend time with me, but then I realized that, of course, I had college classes on Friday morning and I obviously can't swim. When he said he'd teach me to swim at the club, I liked that idea a whole lot, but I guess this is typical of how driven I can be; I had to learn the basics of swimming before our lesson even began.

I thought for the longest time that I wasn't obsessive about things, but now I realize that I guess I am. I always thought it was just my parents pushing me to be valedictorian, but I guess I was pushing myself just as hard as they were. This desire to be overprepared for everything sometimes just seems to dominate my life.

Thursday night before Marcus' swim lesson, I read everything I could find online on how to learn to swim. Then I went to our bathroom tub, filled it up really high, and practiced blowing bubbles, holding my breath underwater, and how to properly exhale. Later on in my room, I practiced how to kick and make the breaststroke, sidestroke, and American crawl, so just like everything else in my life that I do, I was really, really prepared for the lesson.

Marcus was very sweet, gentle, and patient with teaching me the basics. I didn't have the heart to tell him that I learned the night before how to do everything he taught me. But that's okay. It is true that it's the thought that counts. When he encouraged me to try to float, I felt like I already understood the basics of that, too. He was so gentle with me when he was lifting me up so I could float on my back. I thought the whole floating thing was going to be easy because I was so well-prepared, but then when Marcus let go of me, I started to sink, and I guess I panicked a little and the next thing I knew I swallowed a lot of water.

Marcus lifted me back to the surface and put me on my feet. I still felt like I was choking and I definitely was spitting out water. Marcus kept saying it was alright, that everybody goes through that. I was so embarrassed. I'm so used to doing everything perfectly and not ever failing at something.

"I've got to try floating again," I said. "I can do this."

"This time, I'll support your back the whole time," Marcus said. "Relax, I've got you."

And he did. I was able to float for about 10 seconds before I started to sink. This time, I had enough sense to close my mouth.

"Very good, you're doing just fine," he said. "That's all for the day, though."

Before we left, I made him promise to take me for another swimming lesson next Friday, and he promised he would. Next, we went bowling, and I wasn't prepared for that. But bowling was pretty easy to do, after he showed me the basics. Honestly, though, it's not something I would want to do again. So you throw a ball and knock down something. It just seems pointless. Swimming, though, is excellent exercise and practical, too. I could get into that.

The only thing I was nervous about was going to Marcus' house after bowling. I suggested us doing that before I had time to think about it, which isn't like me. Did I suggest that because I want to keep knowing more about him and meet his family? Maybe so. He is an interesting guy. But what I did was basically invite myself over to his house for dinner, which is not how I do things.

The meeting of the mom event turned out really well, though. She's a bright, articulate career woman—a role model for anyone. We started talking about general things, like what was her major in college and what is mine. Then before I knew it we were talking about current events and politics, and we agreed about everything. I mean, there were some controversial topics brought up and she didn't shy away about giving her opinions, which I really admired, and I agreed with them, too, and said that. I bet when Marcus was younger and messed up, which he did a lot, especially when he was a freshman, she let him have a piece of her mind. Good for her. She made him grow up, which is good for me. I'm not interested in boys where I have to fix the little things ... let alone the important things in life.

His dad had to work late and didn't get home until we were finishing dessert. He sat down at the table while we were eating, and I was impressed with him from the start. Marcus' mom offered to go reheat the dinner, but he said absolutely not, that he would go do it himself. It was nice that she offered, but even nicer that he wouldn't let her do that. That's how a successful marriage should operate. Both couples should be respectful of the other person's needs.

I asked Marcus' dad about his job, and we chatted about that a little while. But then he turned his attention to me and said that Marcus had told them that I planned to be a pediatrician. Very interesting. So he thinks enough of me to tell his parents about me, or they were curious enough about me to ask him, and he wanted to tell them about me. Whichever way it was, it was a good thing and puts all of them in a good light. They wanted to know about me, or Marcus wanted to tell them. Yes, that's very good.

After dinner, Marcus and I went downstairs to the rec room and talked some more. Then I saw that he had a ping-pong table, so I thought why not, let's learn one more sport for the day. Ping-pong is a lot more challenging than I thought. I liked it when Marcus held my arms and showed me the strokes and then kissed me.

I also liked it when he asked me to go to prom with him next month. He apologized with it being such short notice, but it's still a month away, so no problem. I've got to have a nice dress for Mama's wedding in May, so I guess I can wear the same one for both the wedding and prom. A very interesting day.

BIG TESTS

49

LUKE

THE A.P. ENGLISH TEST WOULD BE "GRUELING," MS. ROCHE kept saying. She explained the format very clearly: 60 minutes to answer 55 questions, five passages to read, each passage would have 11 questions to answer. "There will be no time for reflection and rereading a passage," she warned.

Then three short answer questions, 20 minutes total for them. Next would come two hours of writing. There would be three essay questions to answer, and we would have 40 minutes per essay. One question, Ms. Roche said, would likely have us reflecting on something we read, probably on a poem. Scores back in July.

The poem stuff was not good news for me. I really haven't liked most of the poetry we've read in A.P. English 12. That rhyme scheme junk confuses the crap out of me, and the poetry terms are boring. Trying to keep them in mind—and their "application" —ruins the rare poem that I do like, so the poetry prompt could be a real problem.

Ms. Roche added that the second prompt would likely be a passage from a novel and would also likely come from a book we'd read this year. Finally, we would have an argumentative essay to write. There would be several choices for the argumentative essay and would most certainly come from a book we'd read for class.

I felt the second and third prompts would be absolutely no problem for me. I would glide through those things—probably in under 40 minutes. I knew Elly knew too about my weakness in poetry, so she invited me over to her house after school the day before the test. We both felt that the best way to go about cramming those poetry terms into me was for her to call out term after term—and there were a ton of the stupid things—then for her to read poetry passages and I would try to guess which term fit those passages best.

I rode home from school with her, and she suggested that we sit on her front porch to study. I know why. Her father had probably told her that under no circumstances should she bring me up to her room. I would probably "lose control" of myself up there. I bet he said something like that. Of course, there are negatives to us sitting on the front porch together. The neighbors might see us and that could be "embarrassing" to him. Screw him.

We started working on the terms at 4:00. It was agonizingly slow. We were still working on them at 5:30 when her dad got home and walked up the steps. "Big test tomorrow," Elly said cheerfully. He mumbled something, his typical response when I'm around, briefly nodded at me, and marched on through the door.

"Well, that went well," she said and started laughing.

"Yeah, I got a nod today; maybe next time he'll actually speak to me," I said.

"Don't worry about him," she said. "I'm his only girl. He's just overly protective. He'll get used to you eventually. If not, well, too bad for him. Let's get back to work."

We did, but my mind wasn't in it for quite a while. I kept thinking about how would I act toward a guy if one day Elly and I had a teenage daughter and I didn't like the guy. Would I be outwardly rude to the guy, talk to our daughter about why the boy was no good? But would talking like that make the girl dig in her heels and rebel against me? Elly is not outwardly rebelling against her dad; she's just disobeying him. That's just a mild way of saying rebelling, though. All that caused me to have a little sympathy for the old man, but not very much.

We were still at it when Elly's mom brought some sandwiches out at 6:30. We were still at it because I was still having trouble with about a third of the poetry terms. I should have paid more attention to those stupid poetry terms this year. It's going to screw me on the test, I just know it. Finally around 8:00, Elly said, "I think we've done all we can do for today. I'm worn out from this. You'll be okay, tomorrow. Go home and get a good night's sleep. I'll drive you."

"No," I said. "I'll run home. It'll take away some of the tension." The running did help a little, but I still tossed and turned and worried what seemed like all night.

The next day, the test was, well, not all that bad. I mean, it was actually pretty easy. Can you believe that? One of the things I've learned from having the "wisdom" of a senior—I'm being sarcastic, can you tell—is that most of the things I was really worried about in high school ended up not being that big a deal. The things that really screwed things up were things that I wasn't worried about, that I didn't see coming. I bet that's how it's going to be in life, too. Elly and I will be thinking that life is just moving on just like it should be, and we're doing okay on two school teachers' salaries and then all of a sudden the washing machine falls apart and we don't have enough money right away to buy a new one. I can see that kind of stuff cropping up all the time.

Anyway, I breezed through the multiple-guess questions in good shape and the short answer ones were even easier. The poetry essay had to be written about Robert Frost's nature poems, which were about the only poems I liked all year. I really lucked out there. For the second essay, I chose the one for

Macbeth, which we had read in class, and I had really liked. The other question I chose was on *Fahrenheit 451*. I really liked that futuristic dystopian stuff. I'm going to enter college with freshman English taken care of. I really think I aced the test.

50

ELLY

WHY CAN'T MY FATHER SEE WHAT A GOOD PERSON LUKE IS? We were sitting on the front porch when Dad got home from work, and the first thing he did when he saw Luke was scowl. I know Luke had to have seen that look. Later when Luke and I finally finished studying for the A.P. English exam and he left, Dad started complaining.

"Why were you sitting out on the front porch with that boy?" he asked. "Everybody in the neighborhood saw you."

I was trying to control my temper when he said that, but it was hard. I had a lot of anger to get out of me. "You told me he was not to ever come to my room," I said. "You've made it clear that you don't want him at the dinner table or even in the house. Where was I supposed to study with him? Out in the street?

"All we were trying to do was get ready for the most important test we've ever taken. We studied for three hours in plain view of everyone, and he never made a *move* on me as you are always saying. What is your problem with him? I'm going to tell you again what I like best about him. He has the best heart of any boy I've ever met."

Then I just left and went upstairs to my room, but about 10

minutes later, I was still so angry that I came down. I decided I wasn't finished yelling at him. He and Mom were in the living room, and as I got closer I could hear them talking.

"You're making a big mistake," she said. "You're going to drive her away from you. I know Elly, and this is the boy she's chosen. This isn't just some teenage fling. I'm going to say it again. This is the boy she's chosen. You know what else? I think she's chosen very wisely, so you'd better get used to him and change your attitude. Or one day, you'll be hoping that she'll let you back into her life."

I could have just hugged Mom when she said that, and I felt all this tension go out of my body, but then Dad started up again.

"You don't know what you're talking about," he said. "She's 18. What does she know about boys or anything else? That boy will never be able to provide for her."

"As I recall, we started dating when we were 18, our freshman year of college," she said. "And I never went out with any other boys after that. How are those two all that different from us?"

"It's not the same at all," he said. "We were more mature than kids these days. We were..."

Mom then interrupted him. "You were more mature?" she said. "The boy I had to tell that he either had to stop getting drunk at frat parties or we were through. The boy who got put on academic probation his freshman year? That boy was more mature than Luke? Who lives by himself, pays all his own bills, and came over here to study tonight so he can graduate from college in three years so he can get ahead in life.

"Elly is lucky to have him, and he is lucky to have her. I'm going to tell you one last thing, and it will probably just make you madder. Elly told me last month that Luke took her to see some land that his grandfather bought for him. She said Luke wants to live there one day. I'm willing to bet that she wasn't telling me everything about that, and the *everything* part is I bet they've already talked about the two of them living there one day.

"I've seen how those two look each other. I've heard how she talks about him. I've seen how he acts toward her. In her heart, she's married to him already."

Then I heard Mom get up and leave the room. I obviously couldn't see Dad's face at that moment, but I know she left him speechless. Good. I hope he can't sleep all night, or any night, until he comes to his senses about Luke and me.

I went back to my room, looked over that long list of literary terms one more time, and went to bed. I really slept well. The way Mom talked to Dad and is on my side, the self-confidence I have now about school and life that I never had before. All those old fears I used to have are gone. I'm a woman now, not just some dumb, insecure ninth grade girl. I'm going to nail that exam.

The exam was hard, I have to say. One of the first questions on the multiple-choice part went something like this. "In the context in which it appears, the phrase "leaped to the sky" suggests which of the following:

1. The gruesome nature of the Holocaust.
2. A desperate attempt to escape.
3. A defiant liberation of spirit.

The choices were A. I only. B. II only. C. I and II. D. I and III. E. I, II, and III. It was strictly an opinion question written by some anonymous person. How could there be a definite right answer? Then I remembered what Ms. Roche had said about how on the exam you couldn't think literally, that the questions were written by people who were paid to confuse you, so the best way to think about different questions was in a symbolic sense. The best symbolic answer was III, the second best symbolic answer was I, the most literal answer was II, so the answer had to be D. I and III.

After I got through that little crisis, I breezed through the rest of the multiple-choice questions, keeping in mind the whole time what Mr. Roche had said. The short answer questions were easy; Ms. Roche had really prepped us well for that. The three essay questions took a long time, but I have good writing skills. I know I did well on them. I believe I can finish college in three years.

51

MARCUS

I asked Mia to come over to my house after school on Thursday to go over a vocabulary word list that Ms. Roche had given us. The list was of words that might appear in the short answer or essay questions and that we had better know. Of course, when Mom found out about that, she told me to invite Mia over for dinner so that the two of them "could talk some more." I'm glad that Mom likes her.

When Mia and I started going over the words, I was doing pretty good until we got to the word *narcissistic*. I said I didn't know what that meant. She burst out laughing and said, "It describes how you were when you were a ninth grader."

"My brother used to call me an 'insufferable little jerk,'" I said.

"That's pretty close," she said and laughed again. "Basically, it means someone has too high of an opinion of himself."

"Well, thanks for the compliment," I said, pretending that I was deeply hurt.

"Oh, Marcus," she said. "I wouldn't be here right now if you were still a narcissist."

"I guess that it is a compliment," I said, and we both started laughing.

After we went over vocabulary words, we went on to the literary terms. It' amazing to me how science and math are really her thing, but she still has all this incredible knowledge about everything else. How does she keep all that information in her head? Some of those literary terms were really hard. Like who really understands what the term *synecdoche* means, when in real life would you ever use that? I mean, seriously.

But when we came to that term, she said something like, "Oh, yeah, a synecdoche is a figure of speech in which a part is used for the whole or the whole for a part, the special for the general or the general for the special."

Run that by me, again, please is what I wanted to say. But I just nodded my head and said let's get on to the next term. Actually, going over the terms and vocabulary words did help me. It was more than just going over them. Studying that stuff for a couple of hours just made me feel comfortable and confident while I was taking the A.P exam. Although we won't get our scores back until July, I'm sure I did really well.

I'm sure I did even better on the Government A.P. exam. There were two parts: the 55 multiple choice questions that you have to answer in 80 minutes and the four questions in the "free response" section that you have to answer in 100 minutes. The first three of those questions should be answered in about 60 minutes. Question four is the argumentative one, and you should take about 40 minutes with that one because it has to have the most detailed response. I studied some for that test, but I honestly felt I knew the material already because I really enjoy anything that has to do with history.

There were a lot of multiple-choice questions where you had to analyze charts and graphs and things like that. Then there were a bunch of questions about the Constitution and how the Founders did this or that. I got a little mad about some of those questions. The Founders were great men, I get that, and it was clear that the writers of the test wanted to honor what the Founders stood for and how the Constitution and the Bill of Rights were great documents. I get that, too. But what really makes me mad is that a lot of those Founders were okay with slavery, even though a lot of them knew it was wrong. And a lot of those same Founders were okay about not letting poor whites vote, believing that they weren't intelligent enough to make good decisions.

The first three response questions I breezed through were about some kind of consumer fraud case and how that should be handled, then about educational trends and what that meant on a regional basis, and then about separation of church and state and what "Civic Religion" means in court cases. No problem with any of those.

But the argumentative essay question got right back to the Founders again and whether they wanted a "participatory, pluralist, or an elite government system." Well, of course, they wanted an elite one run by them. That's what I've been saying all year in government class. I was fired up enough about that topic already, and I really let out my anger when I was writing the essay. Here was my lead.

"The Founders created one of the most enlightened systems of government ever in the history of man. They established many high-minded ideals that would serve this country well in many ways. In fact, many governments around the world have modelled their system of government on ours. However, the actions of the Founders were not matched by their ideals in at least one important way—their permission of the continuation of slavery.

"Imagine this scenario. While the Founders were working on the Constitution, a ship from Africa, filled with slavers, arrived and made their way to the building where the Founders were housed. The leader of the slavers announced that he would be apprehending all of the Founders and taking them to Africa to become slaves. These actions were not personal, mind you, the head slaver said, but the Founders were desperately needed so that the slavers would not need to perform this hard physical labor and so they might become rich black men.

"Furthermore, the wives and children of the Founders were

desperately needed as well, said the head slaver. He said the wives were critically needed as breeders of future slaves, and the children could be sold to faraway plantations so that the slavers could increase their wealth. From time to time, the Founders' wives might also need to be sold to faraway plantations. The head slaver said surely the Founders would have no problem with this because they had basically set up a similar system in America."

And so my argumentative essay went. I was pretty proud of it.

52

MIA

When Marcus told me what he had written for his argumentative essay on the A.P Government exam, I was absolutely stunned. If the person grading that felt the Founding Fathers were perfect, then they would take it out on Marcus and give him a poor grade—ruining his chance of getting a college credit.

On the other hand, I really admired what he did. I've spent a lot of time studying—and reflecting—during my four years of taking advanced history-related classes. Many of these men that were leaders were great and did awesome things, but they were often flawed in various ways. That's not knocking these men, but too many people look upon past leaders unrealistically. It's like they are idealizing these men without thinking things through.

I told Marcus all that, about how I both admired and was concerned about what he had written. He agreed with me that a certain kind of grader would "nail him," but he also said that he gave somebody with an open mind "something to think about." Then he said some of those historic figures did need to be reevaluated. I asked him who was most in need of that and he said Andrew Jackson.

"The man practiced genocide against Native Americans,"

Marcus said. "Jackson pushed the Indian Removal Bill of 1830 which was pure genocide. Even a lot of congressmen back then knew that the bill was morally wrong, but not enough voted their consciences to stop it.

"Jackson also said that whites were the superior race, and he was going to make Indians disappear from the planet. And that man's face is still on the twenty dollar bill. Give me a break."

Wow was all I kept thinking while he was ranting—and I mean ranting in a good way. There's a lot of depth to Marcus that I would never have realized if we had not started dating, and I told him that, too.

My argumentative essay took the form of how the Founding Fathers "set the tone for future American leaders." It was grammatically perfect with perfectly written sentences and perfectly constructed paragraphs, and as usual, I'm sure I'll get one of my perfect grades on it. I always do, but my essay didn't have the depth or meaning like Marcus' did.

Next month, I'm going to have to give my valedictorian speech to the graduating class. Lately, I've been thinking about what I want to write and say. The principal told me he was sure that I wouldn't write anything controversial, but school system policy required that he preview the speech before I give it. I understand and respect that, and I understand and respect the position he is in. Nothing too controversial, get the speeches and songs out of the way, get the seniors across the stage with their diplomas in hand, polite applause every now and then. A couple of fools in the back rows will sound off on their air horns every now and then, but no big deal, and everybody goes home happy.

But what if I gave the seniors and everybody present something to think about? What if I talked about some of the prejudice I put up with, especially when I was a freshman and was one of only about 20 Hispanic kids in the school? What if I spoke about some of the things that were said to me and how they still hurt? Back then, I put those things out of my mind. I didn't want to dwell on them. I never talked to anyone about them, except Hannah and Camila, plus Luke when we were together. Those demons are still racing around in my head. Maybe I should get rid of them before I leave high school.

I've kept my mouth shut for four years and been Ms. Perfect Mexican Girl. I have cultivated this image of myself as mature and as a role model, but should I have been more out there?

After finishing the two A.P. exams, I asked Marcus to take me to the club and give me another swimming lesson. What I really wanted to do, though, was after we had the lesson was to share all these thoughts with him about what I should say.

"That's a tough call," he said. "I mean, if you say what you want to say, the principal might not approve it. But on the other hand, a lot of the things you want to say need to be said. I say go for it. Write out what you want to say and give it to the man. The worst he can do is reject it. He's not going to withhold the diploma from the school valedictorian no matter what. Something like that would make national news, and no principal would want that."

I really thanked Marcus for his advice. But then all of a sudden, he said he wasn't through with his advice.

"Follow your heart," he said. "Say what needs to be said." Then he grinned at me and said. "Give the speech you want to give and nobody will fall asleep, that's for sure."

I'm still not sure what I'm going to do for my speech. I've got to think a lot about this. There's just so much happening right now. Mama's getting married soon. I'm leaving high school soon, prom's coming up, and I've got my college exams to prepare for. But I've got a great, new boyfriend to support me and some really good friends.

PROM

53

LUKE

EVERYBODY IN FIRST PERIOD ENGLISH WAS OBSESSED FOR LIKE months about the A.P. test, but as soon as that was over, the big topics became prom and graduation. I've never cared anything about going to prom when I was a junior or a senior, but the closer it came to the "big dance," the more I worried that maybe Elly wanted us to go. That she would feel deprived somehow if we didn't. I noticed her listening to and talking to the other girls in class about what they would be wearing, so one day during lunch I asked her if she wanted us to go.

"No way," she said. "I've been to three proms and that's enough."

"But you seemed like you were really into what Paige and Leigh and all those other girls were going to wear," I said.

"Of course, I was," she said. "I'm still a girl. I still want to know what everybody's wearing, but I've got other things on my mind now."

"Like what?" I said.

"Well, I think we should go online and get our summer school schedules as coordinated as possible," she said. "We could carpool if we had pretty much the same hours and we could save money on gas. I know you're going to work on campus this summer, but maybe you could work part-time before school lets out to get some extra money. I've just been thinking of things like that. Of course, I'm going to work at the country club again like last summer. Oh, one more thing. Maybe we should call and see if we could get somebody to map out now exactly what courses we would need to take each summer and during the three school years to graduate early and get our teaching certificates."

She was right, so I asked her to get out her phone and we could look online and see when the courses were going to be held. Right there in the cafeteria, she arranged for us to go to the college the Friday before prom to talk to the education department dean who would be our advisor. He could help us get our schedules straight. Friday, the dean helped us pick out our two summer school classes, Biology 101 and Creative Writing.

I felt really good about that. Biology is the science I like best by far, and I figured that college biology would be really hard and would require a lot of study time, but I can handle it. I felt the Creative Writing would be fun and easy and would be something where I could whip out the assignments, so the two classes would really balance each other out. Being an English major, I need to load up on some English electives anyway to make me more hirable when I graduated.

Next, we went to the financial aid office where we met the person Elly had set up for us to see. He said I would have to formally apply for a job, but the college was really in need of grounds workers for the summer: mowing, maintenance, painting, things like that. When I told him I used to run a lawn-mowing business, he joked and said I was probably overqualified for the job. He all but guaranteed that I could find a job on the grounds crew "with my background."

All things considered, it went really well. Elly and I will go to biology class every morning at 8 and spend most of the morning there and in labs. Then I will work on the grounds crew all after-noon, and she'll go to the club to take kids on nature walks and stuff. Then after dinner, she'll drive back to the college for our

Creative Writing class at night. We can work on our biology homework at the school library after we eat dinner and before we go to class.

When we were driving home from getting our summer schedules all set up, I was feeling pretty good about things. Then I started to worry that maybe all this nose to the grindstone stuff might be too much, too hard, on Elly. Me, it's different. It's been like this for me forever. I've never had anything. But now I can see that three years from now, I'll maybe have more than I ever hoped of having: a wife, a house, a job—a good life. All things that I never thought were possible.

When Elly drove me back to my house, I decided to tell her about my hopes and fears, especially the fear that all this was going to be awfully hard on her.

"Luke, I want you to stop thinking that way," she said. "I've found the boy I'm going to be with forever. It's going to be hard the next three years, but then before you know it, it will be over. Look how fast our four years in high school went. This college thing is only three years...look at it that way. Besides."

"Besides what," I said.

"Besides, I love you, you stupid lawn mower boy. You just had to tell them you were an expert lawn mower. You probably could have had some cushy summer job, but, no, you had to tell them about your lawn-mowing expertise."

"I love you, too, Miss Priss," I shot right back. "You should have told them about your previous job skills. What exactly are they again?"

We both started laughing, and then Elly said she had something else on her mind. Of course, I wanted to know what it was. She asked if the river was warm enough now to float, and I said it was.

"Okay, then," she said. "I want you to take me canoeing on prom Saturday. I want to prove to myself that I won't overturn that boat like I did last fall. I want to fix us a lunch to eat out there on the river. Then I want us to go out for ice cream that evening after we get off the river."

"I'll do all those things on one condition," I said.

"What is it?" she said.

"That Sunday, I take you somewhere you've been wanting to go," I said. "A trip that is all about your interests, not mine."

"Deal," she said.

54

ELLY

So on prom Saturday, do I spend all day glamming myself up? You know, getting my artificial tan, artificial nails, sexy gown, and impossibly perfect hair all ready to dazzle some guy? Isn't a girl's senior prom supposed to be one of her all-time nights to remember? I lived for going to prom when I was a freshman and sophomore. My junior year I just went because I had nothing better to do, and now that I'm a senior, I didn't even want to go. I guess, once more, it shows how I have changed—a lot.

Of course, it was awfully sweet for Luke to ask me if I wanted to go to prom. That shows he was putting my feelings first, and that's always nice, but I honestly told him I didn't want to go. He has been so good to me that I wanted to do something nice for him. I know how much he likes being outside, so I suggested we go floating on the river. It made me happy to make him happy.

I have to admit that I was thrilled that he wanted us to do something on Sunday that was all about pleasing me. The past year, Mom has been showing me how to quilt, and I've really enjoyed learning how. You really have to concentrate and pay attention, and it's frustrating when you mess up. Still, at the same time, it's so different from school and studying, which makes it a great stress reliever. It's fun, too, so I asked Luke to take me to quilt shops, and I'd look for patterns, fabric, and stuff. Most importantly, we'll be together, I told him. He smiled and kissed me when I said that.

The Saturday canoe trip was nice. I'm a girly girl, I know that. I'm never going to be really in to all the outside stuff that's so important to Luke. Still, being out there on the river made me feel close to him. He reviewed the strokes that he tried to teach me last fall, told me what to do if we got caught on a mid-river rock (basically just not panic and let him take over), and explained what lures we would be using: tubes, crankbaits, top waters, and jerkbaits. The tube thing was confusing. I mean, don't some people float down a river in a tube? How could that be a lure, too? I decided not to worry about it. He had fun explaining fishing to me, and that was good enough.

I ended up even catching a fish. Luke tied this top water thing on my line and told me just to "cast it out and let it sit." That seemed simple enough. Well, this fish Luke called a "redbreast" came up and just smacked that thing. Luke yelled out to bring it in, that I had "a nice one on," so I took that meant to turn that reel around and around, and the next thing I knew this fish was flopping around in the bottom of the boat. Luke was yelling "awesome" over and over and he was so happy.

I asked him to paddle the canoe over to the shore. I got out my phone and took a selfie of the fish, Luke, and me and told him that I was going to post it on Instagram as soon as we got somewhere where there was cell service. All my female friends will be posting pictures of them and their dates and everybody'll look great. Then they'll look at the picture of the "three of us" on the river: a flopping fish, Luke, and me. I wouldn't swap places with any of them.

We had a really nice lunch out on the river. After I caught my redbreast, Luke said we were going to add fish to the menu. He caught three sunfish about the size of mine while we were on the shoreline. "You know," he said. "Let's just eat lunch here. We've got fresh fish," so we did. Luke built a fire. I stir-fried some asparagus in one pan, and he filleted the fish, put them inside aluminum foil, and roasted them in the coals. I had made an apple pie the night before and put slices for both of us in the cooler. It was really a simple meal, but it was delicious. I took selfies of us eating, too. I love him so much. Even simple things with him are special.

That evening we were tired, my hair was a mess, and my tennis shoes were wet, but I took another selfie of us eating ice cream cones at this little country store near the river. I teased him about my big prom night dinner out with him and how he was such a big spender that he had really impressed me. He laughed so hard at that that I thought he would never stop. I like to make him laugh. I like it when he calls me Miss Priss and makes fun of me. He dropped me off at my house around 7:30, and I had showered and was in bed by 8:00. I was just worn out. Me going to sleep at 8 on senior prom night. Who would have ever thought that?

Our driving to a couple of quilt shops Sunday afternoon was just as special. Luke tried really hard to take an interest in the patterns, threads, and all the paraphernalia that you need when you quilt. It made me happy that he wanted to learn about my new hobby. Since he drove on Saturday, I drove on Sunday and when were done visiting the two quilt shops, I took him back to his house and made him dinner out of what was in his fridge. All I did was warm up deer burgers, mashed potatoes, and peas, but even a simple meal is special with him. It was the best "prom weekend" I've ever had.

MARCUS

THE WHOLE TIME MIA AND I HAVE BEEN DATING, SHE HAS constantly shown how different she is from other girls. A couple of days before prom, I asked her what she was going to do to get ready for it. I was just making conversation. She said, "Study for my college exams and fill out some applications for summer jobs."

Most girls would be getting pedicures and manicures, making hair appointments, and maybe buying some sort of last-minute accessory or something. Not her. I guess maybe I had a puzzled look on my face when I asked her about her preparation, so she said in this really serious tone: "Oh, I understand now, Marcus, you think I need to do something extra to be pretty for you Saturday night. Well, I'm taking a bath Saturday afternoon and shampooing my hair. What more do you want?"

I started stuttering that I hadn't meant to offend her. Then she started laughing.

"I'm teasing you, Marcus," she said. "I do want to look nice for you, but my family's never had enough money for me to have my hair or nails done, and I'm not going to start now. I'll wear my hair down like I always do. I've already ordered a boutonniere for you, and I'll pick it up Friday after school. That's all I really have time to do as far as prepping for prom."

When she talks like that, I'm even more attracted to her and I told her that. She's a natural beauty; she probably even knows that, but she would never say it out loud if you know what I mean. She gives off this self-confidence that is, man, just amazing to be around. When I picked her up Saturday night, she did look awesome. I had asked her earlier if she wanted us to go out for dinner instead of eating what was being served at prom. All she said was she didn't see any point of going out when the meal was already being provided for us. Typical of her.

Dinner was great. We had a mixed green salad to start. Then we had a choice of chicken parmesan, lobster macaroni and cheese, or shoulder tender steak. Mia told me she was ordering the lobster entrée because she liked it so much the one time she had it. Again, I was reminded of how poor her family has always been and how she'll be moving into a totally different world when her mom gets married next Saturday. I know she'll never change her outlook on things, no matter how well-off she becomes from living in my neighborhood or having a successful career.

Mia knows so much about so many important things, but she knows very little about things that most kids our age are all about. Right after dinner, I asked her if she wanted to dance, and she said she didn't know any of the dance moves and I'd have to show her. She also didn't know any of the current songs that all the other kids are into. Freaking amazing. I guess she could tell that I was surprised about all that.

"Marcus, I listen to NPR or some other news station when I'm driving," she said. "I just feel that I need to know what's going on in the world."

Can you believe that? It's like this girl skipped childhood and went straight to being an adult when she turned 14. Later in the night, the DJ went all retro and played some songs from the 1970s like "YMCA" and "Play that Funky Music, White Boy." Mia actually knew those songs, and I had to ask her how.

"Because back in Ms. Hawk's tenth grade English, someone did a PowerPoint on the top songs of the decade when we were studying the '70s."

She remembered a PowerPoint that another student gave over two years ago? No wonder she's the valedictorian and has never made below an *A*.

At 9:00, it was time to do the Senior Lineup. The theme for prom was Starlit Night, so when us seniors came strolling through in front of everybody, the lights were dimmed and all these fake stars were sort of glimmering above us. It was pretty cool. At 9:30, the juniors had planned for an ice cream sundae buffet, so the music stopped for a little while and we had a chance to talk.

"Something's on your mind, Marcus, what is it?" she asked.

I hesitated for a little while. Then I told her what I had been thinking about. That often when we go do something or are talking, I feel a more than a little intimidated by her. She knows so much about so many important things, and I worry that she'll think I'm not somebody that will have, I guess, adult conversation-like talk with her.

"Marcus, you underestimate yourself," she said. "Back when you were a freshman, you constantly overestimated your *charms*. Now, you don't know how much you have to offer some girl. I don't go out with dumb, immature guys. Believe me, I'm very impressed with you. Actually, I'm hoping you'll want to keep seeing me when we're in college next fall."

I kissed her when she said that, and she gave me a big smile back. "Count on that," I said.

"Now, I've got a big favor to ask you," she said.

"Name it," I said.

"Be my date for Mama's wedding next Saturday," she said. "It's a special day for Mama, my sisters, and me, and I want you to be a part of it."

I told her I would be glad to go with her. I'd be glad to do anything with her.

56

MIA

I REALLY DID HAVE A NICE TIME GOING TO THE PROM WITH Marcus. He looked so sexy and sophisticated in his black tux and bowtie. For me, the most stressful thing was finding a gown to wear that we could afford and that could double as a dress for Mama's wedding. She and I agonized for a couple of weeks over about what to buy. Sometimes Mama would say that we shouldn't worry about the expense of anything anymore because Sai was so well-off and we could afford things that we never had before. Then both of us would start agonizing all over again about whether Sai would be upset with us for spending so much money on a gown that likely would only be worn twice all year.

I don't know Sai all that well, but he does seem to be a good man, not the type that would throw a fit over something like a dress. But I think, I know, Mama and I are still, maybe *traumatized is* the word, about how my father was about money, especially the last two years he and Mama were married. How long does it take to wash away the fear that that man inflicted on our family? We haven't heard from him for months. Good!

Mama and I finally bought a lacy keyhole halter dress with a jersey skirt for under a hundred dollars. It was the type of gown that looked more expensive than it was. Know what I mean? It was modest enough for Mama and slinky enough to make me feel sexy, so there was no arguing about anything.

I feel so on top of things when I'm in classes and labs and interacting with my teachers or professors, but I felt socially awkward at prom. I didn't know any of those dance steps, the music was too loud, and the song lyrics were ridiculous the few times I could actually understand what was being sung. The whole prom was like the title of that Shakespeare play we read in English A.P., *Much Ado About Nothing.*

Still, Marcus was really sweet all night, and I did really, really enjoy being with him. He was tender in the way he held my hand and kissed me several times—the way he tried to show me how to dance, without much success, that's for sure. We had planned to go to after prom, but by the time prom ended at 11:30, all I could think of was how tired I was. Also, was I awake enough to go home and get in a little studying before I fell asleep?

High school is all but over with the A.P. exams out of the way, but the week after prom was all about two high stakes college exams. I had Bio 205 General Microbiology on Monday. The genetics, ecology, and physiology part of the class are really easy to understand, but the morphology aspects require a lot of thought and time to fully comprehend them, so I knew I had to spend a lot of time going over my notes and labs on that. After Marcus kissed me goodnight at midnight, which was really romantic, I studied until about 2:00 A.M. before I fell asleep. I should never have studied while lying down on the sofa.

I didn't have any college classes on Monday morning, so I spent most of that time going over my bio notes again. In fact, I spent most of my time at high school that afternoon looking over those notes. I was super prepared for the test on Tuesday morning. None of the questions or topics threw me.

After the exam, I went straight home and started studying for the Chemistry 112, College Chemistry II exam. I already knew the fundamental laws and theories from part I. The second semester was basically how to apply those things. I feel like I aced that exam, just like the bio one. And just like that I was through with college for the semester.

I drove home and just wanted to sleep for like 20 hours, but when I got there Mama was in a tiz about the wedding. She was having some sort of crisis about her wedding gown. Did it show too much cleavage, would Sai like it, on and on. It wasn't like her to be acting that way. Mama hadn't had this big of a meltdown since she learned that because she and my father had divorced but had never got their marriage annulled by the church, that the two of them were still married "in the eyes of the church." At least, that's what the priest said. Then the man offered to give Mama and my father counseling for a "blessed reconciliation."

Mama told the priest that it was her husband that had abandoned the family, not the other way around. All the priest kept saying was "What did you do to drive him away?" Obviously, Mama's wedding ceremony was not held in our Catholic church. Actually, we haven't been back there since Mama stormed out of the priest's office.

My sisters and I spent much of Thursday and Friday afternoons working with the movers to get our things over to Sai's house and into our new rooms. It was a little sad to leave what had been our home for six years, giving our chickens away to a neighbor, saying goodbye to our neighbors. In Sai's neighborhood, an ordinance "forbids fowl of all descriptions." Absolutely ridiculous.

Mama did look so beautiful on Saturday, and my prom gown was perfect for the ceremony. I'm so glad Marcus was there to accompany me. He was very attentive to me and even joked about protecting me from all of Sai's fellow doctors that were there. Right after the wedding, Sai and Mama left for a weeklong honeymoon to Bermuda. It was really weird to drive my sisters in a car that we hadn't bought to a house that was like a mansion where for a week I would be the oldest person in it. Before he left, Sai told me I was "in charge of the place" until he and Mama got back. More weird stuff. I spent much of the rest of the weekend working on my graduation speech.

GRADUATION

57

LUKE

I THINK THERE ARE SOME DAYS IN LIFE WHERE YOU'LL ALWAYS remember just about everything about them. That's the way last Monday was for me—the day I graduated from high school. Some of the day was surreal, some of it was a little sentimental, some was a little unbelievable, some of it was boring—but the last part was wonderful and special.

The day sort of started on Sunday night. Elly called me and said her mom wanted to fix an "honoring the graduates" breakfast for us on Monday morning around 8:30. Elly said she would drive over and pick me up to take me to her house. We had already planned to spend the day together, so I thought why not. I was a little worried about Elly's dad being around when we got there, so I asked about that. Elly said he always leaves for work by 8:15. Well, that makes sense why breakfast was at 8:30.

The surreal part of the day was sitting at the family table with Elly's mom waiting on us. The breakfast was fantastic: waffles with blueberry compote and lemon ricotta cream. I kept wondering why Elly's mom was doing this. I mean, it was awfully kind of her. It was only after we left for graduation practice at school that Elly told me why her mother had wanted me over.

"Mom told me it was her way of letting you know that she approves of you, of us as a couple."

It was me who wanted for us to get to school by 9:30. Since graduation practice in the auditorium was not until 10:00, Elly wanted to know why. The seniors haven't had to go to classes since last Thursday. Friday morning was senior awards today. Spoiler alert. I didn't get any, absolutely shocking! One last little bit of senior sarcasm. And on Monday, most of the juniors and sophomores skipped school. Only the freshmen came on that next to last day of school. They're pretty clueless about things. I know I always was at that age.

Anyway, the reason I wanted to come early was, I guess, sentimental. With the classrooms practically empty of students and "no learning" going on, I wanted to go visit my favorite teachers one last time and say something from my heart to them —thank you. I had Ms. Hawk all four years I was there, and Elly and I went there first. I told her she was the first teacher that believed in me and I really appreciated that, that she was one of the people that turned around my life. And she said something to us that made Elly tear up and made me almost do it.

"I'm glad you two finally found each other," Ms. Hawk said. "You are really good for each other. Please e-mail me next year and let me know how you're doing in college."

Then we went to Ms. Roche and thanked her for teaching us in English the last two years. I told her she was hard but got me ready for college, and I was grateful for that. Next, it was on to Mr. Wayne's room. I told him that he had given me an interest in history and was one of the reasons that I might try to minor in it if my schedule worked out. After that, we went to Mr. Martin's room, and I thanked him for making us do all that project-based learning and how it had prepared me for college. Last, we went to Mr. Caldwell's office. I thanked him for being patient with me all those times I was sent to the office my freshman and sophomore years. I told Caldwell I knew he was "never out to get me," that he just wanted me to succeed. It's true what they say: good teachers can make a difference in your life. That's a big reason why I want to be one.

Graduation practice was boring, so enough about that already. Lunch was the unbelievable part of the day. After practice, Elly said she had gotten a text from Mia inviting us to go out to lunch for pizza with her and Marcus. Marcus and I have become really good friends. Probably he and Allen are the only guys from high school I'll try to stay in touch with. People say that you lose touch with just about everybody that you went to high school with, that "life gets in the way." Spouses, kids, jobs, the day to day. I bet that's true, don't you think?

I've barely talked to Mia since that time she came over, but I'm glad she wanted to say goodbye to me by having the four of us eat out together. I'm glad that she and Marcus are together. Man, they could be a power couple in life if things came down to that. I'm also glad that after lunch, she came over and hugged me and whispered a few things to me. It was good to see and talk to her. After graduation, who knows if that will ever happen again?

Graduation was the other boring part of the day. It was so, what's that literary term, anticlimactic? I didn't listen to hardly anything that was going on until the principal started calling out the graduates' names. Well, of course, I listened to Mia's speech. You couldn't not pay attention to that...powerful stuff! Most of the time my mind was on a thousand other things: hurry up and get this thing over with, I've got to start work at the college tomorrow doing maintenance "patrol," I've got to buy my college textbooks, Elly, Elly, Elly. Right before she got up to go get her diploma, she turned around and gave me this little flirty smile and wink. I love it when she does stuff like that. When she smiles at me, there's nothing better in life.

After graduation, we went to my house and sat out on the porch until around midnight, just talking and holding each other. I'm going to have a wonderful life with the person I love. I know that I've got a lot of hard work ahead of me, ahead of us, but things are going to work out just fine. I've got all these hopes and dreams, and they're really going to come true.

58

ELLY

GRADUATION WAS ONE OF THE BEST DAYS OF MY LIFE. IT ALL started with Mom making breakfast for Luke and me after Dad left for work. Before Luke got here, I asked her if Dad knew that Luke was coming over. She said she had told Dad about the breakfast and all he did was "grumble a little, which is real progress." He's coming around, Mom said, time is "on our side." Mom *is* on my side about Luke and me, which is really important to me.

I really admired Luke for wanting to go visit our favorite teachers before graduation practice. The kind heart he has is always showing itself. I think it's because he has never had much of anything in life. That's why he's very appreciative when people show him kindness. Graduation practice was pretty boring, but so what. My mind was elsewhere the whole time, so probably was everybody else's. If you're too stupid to figure out how to "line up," after 13 years in school, you probably shouldn't be graduating anyway.

I was really surprised when I got a text from Mia asking if Luke and I might want to go out to lunch with her and Marcus. I haven't talked to her as much this year except during those sleepovers, and I've really missed that. I know it's a little awkward with us both having had the same boyfriend. After the text, I called her, and we talked for about an hour. She raved about Marcus and how great he was, and I agreed. Finally near the end of the conversation, she said, "Listen, I just wanted to say again that I'm happy for you and Luke. I really, really mean that. I knew if the two of you ever got together, it would be wonderful."

"It is," I said. "We've talked about...," then I hesitated because I didn't know if Luke would mind if I finished that statement.

"Marriage?" she asked.

"Yes," I said. "In three years, when we graduate early from college."

"I'm not surprised," she said. "I bet he's taken you to the land his grandfather bought for him to live on."

"Yes, we've talked about where to build a house," I said.

"You tell him I'm happy for you both," she said.

"Why don't you tell him that," I said.

"You wouldn't mind?" she said.

"Of course not," I said. "You know me better than that."

"I just might, then," she said.

After lunch with Marcus and Mia, I went home and slept most of the afternoon. I didn't realize I was so tired from all that end of high school/get ready to go to college rush. When it came time for dinner, I barely ate anything. I was just so excited about graduation. Plus, I was in a hurry to go pick up Luke and get to the civic center. I ended up getting to his house at 5:15, even though I hadn't needed to get there until 5:40 or so. We didn't have to be at the civic center until 6:00. Why on earth did we have to be there so early when we didn't have to line up until 6:50? Just one last, little, silly, high school rule.

It really was a wonderful ceremony. The band played the prelude music, and then we all marched in to "Pomp and Circumstance." Mom and Dad had told me where they were going to try to sit, so I was looking for them when I walked in. I glanced up and saw them, and Mom waved and Dad grinned. My brothers just sat there like knots on a log. They complained all day about having to go...typical.

As class president, Paige welcomed everybody, and then the superintendent and principal did their things. Next, the choir sang "The Climb," that Miley Cyrus song about uphill battles that we'll have to overcome. I honestly had been looking forward all day to what Mia was going to say during her valedictorian speech. I was more than a little surprised, shocked really, about some of the things she said, but they sure were powerful. Kylee spoke next as the salutatorian. Her speech was excellent, too.

Graduation was great, but the best part of that long day was going over to Luke's house and rocking in his front porch swing with him until midnight. I want one of those in our house, and I told him that. He laughed and said, "We can take this one when we go. I mean that. It'll be something to remind me of Granddaddy. We used to sit in it and rock and talk when I was little."

It must have been three hours that we spent doing that. Sometimes we talked; sometimes we just rocked. I think we must have dozed off a couple times. It was so quiet and peaceful, me resting my head on his shoulder, his arms wrapped around me. The last time we woke up, it was nearly midnight. I told Luke that I was so tired that I didn't know if I could drive home. He said he would drive me and then walk home. I protested and he said, "No, I'll do it. I'll take care of you...always."

"Promise," I said, and he just grinned.

I know that he always will.

59

MARCUS

Guys aren't supposed to feel sentimental or melancholy or whatever the word is when you're moody and reflective all day, but that's how I felt the whole time on graduation day. I'll probably never set foot in the school again. I'll probably never see 95 percent—or more—of my class members again. I'll probably never come to a high school reunion. I'll probably end up with a job at some museum or university hundreds of miles away.

I've seen how things are with Joshua when he comes home from college. He spends most of his time with his fiancé Jordan. He always says when I call him that we'll go shoot hoops or do some talking when he comes home, but it almost never happens. Not because he doesn't want it to. It's just by the time he and Jordan hang out, he finishes his studying and talks to Mom and Dad some, there's just not much time for anything else. When he and Jordan graduate, there's no telling where they'll be living or how stressful their jobs and lives will be. I'll get to talk to him even less then. It's not his fault or mine. I guess it's just life.

Before graduation practice and before I met up with Mia, I had three last stops to make at school. First, I went to Coach Dell. I figured he would be sitting in his tenth-grade health class watching clips from last season. Sure enough he was. Teachers, students, nobody does much school stuff the last two days. I just wanted to tell him how much I respected him as a coach and I thanked him for the opportunity to play for him. He told me he really appreciated that.

I then went to Coach Henson and told him if by chance I ever got into basketball coaching at any level, from rec leagues for elementary kids or whatever, he would be my role model on how to work with young people. Henson replied that if I came back to this area to work after college, he would like to hire me as an assistant coach. That's one of the nicest things anybody has ever said to me, but I just can't see coming back to this area to live. You never know, though.

Finally, I went to visit Mr. Wayne, telling him that he was the main person that gave me a love for history. I told him that I had gone from getting caught cheating on a history test as a ninth grader to majoring it in college as a career choice. He laughed and said, "That's quite a roundabout route to take." He was right about that, for sure.

I was really glad that Mia wanted us to go out for lunch with Luke and Elly after graduation practice. Luke's one of the few guys I'm going to try to stay in touch with after high school. I know Elly has been one of Mia's best friends, but things have been a little weird between them after the word got out that Luke and Elly were a thing. Mia just said she wanted to set things right before graduation, which makes sense to me. It also made sense to me that she wanted to say something in private to Luke after lunch. Mia even asked me if I minded if she took just a minute to say goodbye to Luke. I told her of course not. She said the sweetest thing to me after she came back from saying bye to Luke.

"I only had two great boyfriends in high school," she said. "My first one and my last one. I hope that last one will still be there for me when I go off to college."

When I picked up Mia to go to graduation, I could tell the valedictorian speech thing was still really weighing on her mind. So I said, "I'm willing to bet you're still thinking about your speech tonight. Do you want me to look over it? I'm really curious about what you're going to say, anyway."

"I didn't finish making changes in it until this morning," she said. "The principal read it yesterday morning. I think he was a little worried about it, but he approved it. He even said that some of the things I wrote needed to be said."

Her speech was super impressive. I'm not surprised. Everything about her is impressive. I'm glad she probably made some of the seniors uncomfortable. They definitely needed to be made that way, if they even bothered to listen to her when she talked.

After graduation ended, Mia and me ran into Caleb and Mary on our way out. They were arguing over something and both of them were spewing out some of their favorite four-letter words. Talk about two people who deserve each other. When Caleb saw me, he stopped arguing for a second so that he could shoot me the finger. I just kept walking. When we passed by them, I heard him mouth off the n-word and make a comment about Mia's ancestors. "Did they swim or wade across the Rio Grande?"

Mia flinched when he said that, but I just held her hand tighter and whispered, "Keep walking." When we got to my car, I told her that Caleb wasn't worth an insult and added, "What just happened will probably be one of the top 10 moments of Caleb's life after high school. Let him be big man on campus one last time."

"You're right," she said. "Where to, now?"

"How about coffee and conversation at my house," I said. "Then when we're through with that. I'll walk you home. You're only five houses down."

And that's how graduation night ended and the rest of my life began. Who knows where I'll be or what I'll be doing five, ten years from now, but I hope Mia will somehow be a part of it.

MIA

I WAS GLAD THAT MARCUS DIDN'T MIND ME HAVING A MOMENT alone with Luke after we ate lunch with him and Elly on graduation day. They say you never forget your first crush, and I'll never forget Luke. It was very important and meaningful to me to sit around a table and talk to three of the people that were so important to me in high school. After we ate and Luke and I were alone for that little minute, I said, "I just wanted to say goodbye and that I'm very happy for you and Elly. If you ever need somebody to talk to or help in a crisis, you call me, okay?"

"I will," he said. "I hope you'll do the same." Then we hugged one last time.

I'm used to being super self-assured in everything that I do, but giving the valedictorian speech that night was beyond stressful. Here's what I presented on the stage.

"My four years at this school have been the most wonderful ones of my life, and I do think they helped prepare me for my future. I had so many fantastic friends and teachers who helped me along the way so I might have a good future. But before I talk about that wonderful future and what the years may bring to us all, I wanted to talk about some of the bad things that happened.

"On my first day here, somebody told me 'Why don't you go back to where you came from?' I was a little naïve back then. I kept thinking, how did that guy know I was from Texas? I'm going to pause a little bit to let you know that is my way of telling a little joke. Go ahead and laugh if you want to. It wasn't until later in the day that I realized that the guy had seen a *Mexican*, 'Oh, the horror,' felt threatened by it, and mouthed off. As you know, some people say most of us are murderers and rapists, so he naturally thought I was one, too, and here also 'to steal his job.' We Mexicans, you know, will steal anything not bolted down.

"It's not just evil Mexican teenage girls that are a threat to people like that. One of my best friends here is gay and since she is still only semi-out, I'm not going to mention her name. The things she has had to put up with it: the taunts, the profanity, the ugly looks are things that no high school student should have to deal with.

"And it's not just 'people not from around here' or people who are gay or bi or 'different' in some other way. I also witnessed rude comments toward people who were so-called lower class or poor white trash. One of the great things about America is that people can work hard and achieve and better themselves, no matter where they start out in life, class-wise. I think some of you need to learn that fact.

"Enough with the bad stuff. Here's the really good news about the young people at this high school. The people who have said bad things to me and my friends are in the minority here and, I really, really believe this, in schools across the country. I am very hopeful and positive about our generation. I think we are more tolerant, less judgmental, and kinder to others and our peers than the generations that came before us.

"I know that other generations, when they were young, have been idealistic about building a better world. I think as young people we share that idealism, but we also have a healthy dose of realism mixed in...a realism that previous generations probably didn't have, and which made them unhappy, maybe even bitter, when their perfect imagined worlds didn't work out.

"I think we have that realistic outlook because so many of us have come from broken homes and because so many traumatic things have happened in this country and the world during our short lives. The broken home situation is something I can definitely relate to, as I haven't heard from my father in a long time. So we know that struggles are going to happen, bad things are going to occur, and our dreams will be interrupted. But though we possess the realism to understand that our dreams may often be delayed, we also possess the idealism and drive to understand that our dreams will never be crushed.

"Tonight, I want each of you to promise yourself to follow your dreams and never to be discouraged if they don't work out... at first. Because chances are that all the good stuff that we want to happen in life won't happen for years, maybe even many years. If you will just keep striving, though, those hopes and dreams will come true, and your fears will melt away.

"Oh, one last thing. In case that guy who four years ago told me to go back to where I came from is here tonight, I just want him to know that my dream is to become a pediatrician and move back to Texas and practice my profession there. I just thought he would want to know that I finally listened to his advice to go back from where I came from. I hope each and every one of you have your hopes and dreams come true."

THE END

ABOUT THE AUTHOR

Bruce Ingram is a high-school English teacher and lifelong outdoorsman who has written five well-reviewed river guides set in his native Virginia. *Twelfth Grade Hopes and Fears* is the fourth and concluding title in the "American High School" series, which also includes *Ninth Grade Blues*, *Tenth Grade Angst*, and *Eleventh Grade Stress*.